GUIDE FOR SCHOOL-BASED

DRUG POLICY AND

ADVISORY COUNCILS

By:

Isabel Burk, M.S., CHES
The Health Network

The Health Network
New City, New York

Library of Congress Catalog Card Number: 98-74888

ISBN: 0-9655436-5-X

Printed in the United States of America

To order additional copies, contact:

Isabel Burk
(845) 638-3569
(845) 638-1928 FAX
iburk@idt.net
www.healthnetwork.org

Contents

Acknowledgments vi
About the Author vii
Preface viii

Chapter 1   **Purposes and Benefits of School Drug Policy**
   Federal, State or Local Statutes May Require Policies 1
   Policy Sets Clear Boundaries 2
   Policy Encourages Involvement 2
   Policy Unifies Many Stakeholders 3
   Policy Communicates Shared Values,
      Concern and Commitment 3
   Policy Enhances and Supports the Educational
      Mission of School Systems 3
   Policy Defines Individuals' Responsibilities
      and Roles 3
   Policy is Proactive 4
   Policy Provides Written Records and Opportunities
      for Analysis and Revision 4
   Policy Provides Protection in Legal and Procedural
      Issues 4
   Policy Spurs Recognition of Drug-Related Problems 4
   Policy Promotes Prevention 5

Chapter 2   **Developing Policy**
   Leadership 8
   Steps to Policy Development 8
   Checklist 17

Chapter 3   **Essential Components of School Drug Policy**
   Introduction: Rationale and Philosophy 19
   General Statement of School Policy on ATOD 20
   Students and Employees 21
   School Health Education 22
   Prevention 23

Intervention, After-care and Re-entry 25
Resources/Employee Assistance Program 25
Disciplinary Measures/Codes of Conduct 26
Accountability 27
Staff Development 28
Checklist 29

**Chapter 4 Procedures for Implementation
           and Enforcement**
Implementation Training 31
Roles and Responsibilities 31
Pilot-Test and Refinement Procedures 32
Cooperation With Law Enforcement Agencies 32
Fair and Consistent Enforcement 33
Monitoring 34
Review, Modification and Updating 35
Checklist 36

**Chapter 5 Disseminating, Publicizing and
           Promoting Policy**
Begin With Staff 37
Informing Community Agencies 38
Informing Students 38
Public Dissemination 38
Checklist 41

Chapter 6 Issues for Special Consideration
Drug Testing: Students 43
Drug Testing: Employees 44
Drug Policy for Athletes 45
Searching for Drugs 46
Protecting and Preserving Potential Evidence 46

Chapter 7 Assembling a District Advisory Council
Benefits of an Advisory Council 49
Advisory Council Requirements Under ESEA Title IV:
    Safe and Drug-Free Schools Act 49

Drug Advisory Council and the School's Health
  Advisory Council 50
Getting Started/Revitalizing the Drug Advisory
  Council 50
Membership Categories 51
Soliciting Membership 52
Selecting Members 53
Checklist 55

Chapter 8   Advisory Council Roles and Responsibilities

Advisory Capacity 57
Responsibilities Outlined Under ESEA Title IV:
  Safe and Drug-Free Schools Act 58
Scope/Orientation 60
Working Together 61
Minutes/Records 61
Additional Duties or Projects 61
Council Members as Program Advocates 62
Public Relations 62
Reporting Procedures 62
Continuity 63
Checklist 64
Sample Agendas 64

Appendix A 69
  ESEA Title IV Section 4115 (A)(1)(2): Safe and
  Drug-Free Schools and Communities Act
Appendix B 71
  Goals 2000 Part C—Environmental Tobacco Smoke
    (Pro-Children Act of 1994)
Appendix C 73
  Safe and Drug-Free Schools Principles of Effectiveness
Appendix D 77
  Case Histories for District Drug Policy
Appendix E 87
  Resources

Acknowledgments

I gratefully acknowledge the assistance of the following reviewers. The perspective of these professional colleagues was invaluable, and their astute comments, suggestions and editing contributed in no small measure to this final document.

Mr. Jim Ashton, SDFSCA Educational Specialist
Virginia Department of Education

Dr. Arlene Cundiff, Safe and Drug-Free Schools Director
Virginia Department of Education

Mr. Bobby Heard, Executive Director
Mothers Against Drunk Driving

Ms. Ellen Morehouse, Executive Director
Student Assistance Services, Inc.

Dr. Jan Ozias, Editor
School Health Alert Newsletter

Mr. Michael Wessely, Manager
National Education Policy Network
National School Boards Association

I am indebted to my sister and role model, Marian Wood, and my brother-in-law, Wallis Wood, my very first editor, for their continuing advice and guidance. My sister Harriet Burk has believed in me from the very beginning.

I thank my children, Heather and Andrea, for their affirmation and love throughout the development process. They celebrated with me every time a chapter or milestone was completed!

A big thank-you to Bob Bensley, who encouraged and supported me throughout this process.

Isabel Burk
New City, N.Y.
November, 2000

About the Author

Isabel Burk, M.S., CHES, CPP

Isabel Burk, Director of The Health Network, is a nationally known, award-winning expert on health, prevention, and education issues. Her professional achievements have been honored by the U.S. Department of Health and Human Services, Northeast Regional Center for Safe and Drug-Free Schools, Commission for a Healthy New York, and New York State Department of Health. She has made presentations to more than 35,000 people in 32 states, and is a nationally certified health education specialist.

Isabel has been a guest on 20/20 Downtown, CBS This Morning, The View, Phil Donahue show, Good Day NY, WPIX-TV, WNBC-TV, Fox News, WCBS Radio, and WRKL Radio, more.

She chairs the American School Health Association's Council on Alcohol, Tobacco and Other Drugs, and is co-author of New York Office of Children and Family Services' *Innervisions for Youth*, a prevention program for incarcerated youth.

For information on training, program development or technical assistance, please contact:

Isabel Burk
(845) 638-3569
www.healthnetwork.org

Preface

As Regional Safe and Drug-Free Schools Coordinator for 117 districts in New York State from 1989-1996, I noticed that I was responding to similar questions, issues, concerns and training requests by school officials in my service region. When I began working on a consultant basis, school officials across the country expressed very similar needs and concerns, seeking guidance on policy and advisory council matters. This book is the result of many years of professional experience helping schools improve and enhance their drug policies and strengthen their drug advisory councils (DAC).

Some school districts were not aware of the Safe and Drug-Free Schools Act (ESEA Title IV) requirement for a DAC. Others did not know how to assemble, operate or maintain a DAC. I found that in most cases, the talents and skills of this potentially productive group remained relatively unknown and underused.

In the policy arena, I have known of a few unfortunate situations where schools have faced negative consequences, an angry public and threat of legal action because the district's policies or procedures were not clear, up-to-date or appropriately enforced. Some of these troubles could have been avoided through careful planning and an understanding of the *process* of policy development.

After some research, I decided to write a definitive guidebook to help school districts across the country deal successfully with these cornerstones of drug prevention.

What Is This Guide Designed to Do?

Districts using this manual will be able to develop (or upgrade) school drug policies and procedures that are appropriate and useful for their circumstances. Just as each student and staff member is unique, each school district has a different profile of needs that should point the way to policies specific to that community.

Schools cannot stop drug use simply by writing and publishing a policy. The dynamic nature of alcohol, tobacco and other drug (ATOD) issues means that schools must be vigilant and responsive to many factors, with the ability to adjust policies and procedures on an ongoing basis. Therefore, this guide deals with the *process* of policies and procedures: development, implementation, dissemination, monitoring, evaluation and modification.

Suggestions for policy, procedures and legislative mandates are included in the guide, but legal advice is not. Guidance on legal matters should always be obtained from the school district's attorney. Consider the attorney a member of the policy development team who should be consulted at every stage of the process.

This guide covers two related subjects: drug policy and drug advisory councils. Chapters 1-6 are devoted to school drug policies and procedures, and Chapters 7-8 describe the organization and functions of school district advisory councils. These activities can take place at any time, independent of each other. In other words, a school can undertake a drug policy initiative whether or not it has an advisory council, or a school can assemble an advisory council whether or not it has a drug policy. The two go together but can function independently of one another.

Effective drug policy can provide a strong foundation for your school district's drug prevention efforts. When appropriately developed, disseminated and enforced, policy sets the tone for a safe and drug-free school community. But if it is not done properly, the school could find itself open to negative publicity or legal liability.

Likewise, the DAC is a critical component of your drug prevention programming. Its function and influence can range far beyond the mandate set forth by the Safe and Drug-Free Schools Act: the members can be your program's biggest supporters!

If you had a DAC in previous years, use this guide to revive and direct it. With some training and development, you can count on the DAC to serve your district well, working to maintain and expand effective programs, and spreading the good news about your prevention efforts.

Terms Used in This Guide

ATOD	Alcohol, tobacco and other drugs
CSHE	Coordinated school health education
DAC	Drug Advisory Council
DFSCA	Drug-Free Schools and Communities Act
Drug-Free School Zone	Defined by Federal law: 1,000 feet from the perimeter of the school's property boundaries.
EAP	Employee Assistance Program
ESEA	Elementary and Secondary Education Act
FERPA	Family Educational Rights and Privacy Act, a Federal Law that governs disclosure of information from education records.
HAC	Health Advisory Council
IASA	Improving America's Schools Act of 1994
Inhalant substances	Gases, volatile chemicals or solvents that are deliberately concentrated and inhaled to get "high."
Medications	Legal prescription and OTC drugs. These may be addressed in school "drug" policy but also warrant specific medicine administration policy.
NIDA	National Institute for Drug Abuse
NCADI	National Clearinghouse for Alcohol and Drug Information

Paraphernalia	Items or implements to make, use or distribute drugs.
PR	Public Relations
PRIDE	Parents Resource Institute for Drug Education
SDFSCA	Safe and Drug-Free Schools and Communities Act
Student Assistance	A school-based substance abuse counseling program.

Chapter 1

PURPOSES AND BENEFITS OF SCHOOL DRUG POLICY

Why should schools promulgate and promote school policies concerning use, possession and conduct regarding alcohol, tobacco and other drugs (ATOD)? The motivations may be legal, educational, safety, financial or ethical and represent a range of highly visible political and public health issues.

Drugs continue to be a major concern for students, parents, businesses, schools and the community. In the past two decades, schools have become a prime venue for drug prevention efforts. Hundreds of programs, curricula, activities and projects have been developed for use with students from the pre-kindergarten through the senior high school years.

However, education and prevention programs alone will not work. Explicit standards for behavior are needed. Most school districts outline their standards in policy documents that are reviewed and approved by the Board of Education. Drug policies should not be approved, indexed and filed away. They should be dynamic documents that have the potential to impact students, staff and families in a positive, proactive manner.

This chapter outlines the reasons why schools need drug policies, laying a foundation from which effective policy can be written.

FEDERAL, STATE OR LOCAL STATUTES MAY REQUIRE POLICIES

Under the Drug-Free Workplace Act of 1988, all employers (including schools) working with federal contracts or receiving federal funds must adopt a drug-free workplace policy.

According to the U.S. Department of Labor, this act requires that such employers:

1

1. Certify that they will provide a drug-free workplace.

2. Publish a statement notifying employees that the unlawful manufacture, distribution, dispensing, possession or use of a controlled substance is prohibited in the workplace and what actions will be taken against employees for violations.

3. Establish an ongoing, drug-free awareness program to inform about the dangers of drug abuse, the employer's policy, the availability of drug counseling programs and consequences for drug abuse violations in the workplace.

4. Require each employee directly involved in the contract/grant to notify the employer of any criminal drug convictions for violations occurring in the workplace.

5. Notify the federal government of criminal violations.

6. Require consequences for an employee convicted of a drug abuse violation in the workplace.

POLICY SETS CLEAR BOUNDARIES

To establish a positive and orderly school climate, behavioral standards should be explicitly stated, along with expectations and consequences for breaches of these standards. This becomes part of the learning process, setting the tone and delineating the boundaries of appropriate (and legal) conduct. This helps people better understand what they can and cannot do.

POLICY ENCOURAGES INVOLVEMENT

Policy is intended to protect the health and safety of students and employees. For it to be successful and effective, many people must be consulted, included and involved in the process. Collaboration creates a bond and enhances understanding of prevention and intervention issues. Encouraging individuals to work together toward common goals will enhance the educational process and broaden the base of support.

POLICY UNIFIES MANY STAKEHOLDERS

An assembled working committee should engage people from every walk of life. Meeting the needs of increasingly diverse communities obligates the district to involve people with a variety of interests, needs and attitudes. Students and their views should be particularly welcomed because their roles as contributing group members and leaders enhance the process.

POLICY COMMUNICATES SHARED VALUES, CONCERN AND COMMITMENT

A school drug policy can be a powerful statement of values. When policy is developed and publicly promoted, students, employees, families, businesses and community members unite through their common concern for health and safety. A carefully crafted policy can strengthen the school's ability to assist and serve its constituents, and promote healthier lifestyles through prevention and early intervention programs.

POLICY ENHANCES AND SUPPORTS THE EDUCATIONAL MISSION OF SCHOOL SYSTEMS

What can be more vital to the school's educational mission than a safe and healthy school population? Drug-free students are healthier and learn better. Drug-free employees are healthier, more productive and better role models for young people. Respect for self and others, good citizenship and lifelong learning are all ideals that are reflected and supported by a good policy document.

POLICY DEFINES INDIVIDUALS' RESPONSIBILITIES AND ROLES

Any system is only as good as its elements. Apprising students and employees of their roles and responsibilities helps them contribute to a safe and healthy school environment. More importantly, clarifying roles and responsibilities makes everyone in the system accountable.

POLICY IS PROACTIVE

The old adage, "a stitch in time saves nine," is still true. The fact is, sooner or later ATOD will become an issue at school. Thinking ahead and preparing for the foreseeable future is good management practice—and can prevent some difficult predicaments.

POLICY PROVIDES WRITTEN RECORDS AND OPPORTUNITIES FOR ANALYSIS AND REVISION

Policies reflect the laws, values and needs of society, school and community. The dynamic nature of school drug policies necessitates constant monitoring and revision. As laws, values and needs change, policies must be reviewed and modified to keep pace and better serve constituents.

POLICY PROVIDES PROTECTION IN LEGAL AND PROCEDURAL ISSUES

Schools with a clearly stated, written position on drug-related issues are less likely to be involved in protracted hearings, legal wrangling and other time-consuming, expensive situations. In the event of legal action, written procedures provide a paper trail. This points to the need for wide distribution of policy, along with appropriate training for implementation and annual reviews for students, parents and staff.

POLICY SPURS RECOGNITION OF DRUG-RELATED PROBLEMS

Many schools require an ATOD assessment for individuals who violate sections of the drug policy. Others refer violators to the student assistance counselor or a community agency. Intervention, assessment and referral links people with the help they need to be healthy and drug-free.

POLICY PROMOTES PREVENTION

Policy brings prevention to life, just one of many visible reminders that families, schools and the community are committed to working for a drug-free society. Section 4116 (a) of the Drug Free Schools and Communities Act of 1994 requires all schools to design programs to "(A) prevent the use, possession and distribution of tobacco, alcohol and illegal drugs by students and to prevent the illegal use, possession and distribution of such substances by employees; (B) prevent violence and promote school safety; and (C) create a disciplined environment conducive to learning."

Any number of factors can unnecessarily reduce the effectiveness of policy. A poor policy cannot be enforced, an excellent policy cannot work if it is unknown, and a good policy will not work if no one understands, supports or enforces it.

Good policies foster responsibility and respect for self and others. Rather than emphasizing punitive aspects in policy, emphasize the positive! Healthy, clear policies and procedures are messages of caring and support. For these policies to be effective, they must be carefully written and implemented.

Chapters 2-6 of this guide are designed to be used as a blueprint to make your district drug policies successful and effective.

Chapter 2

DEVELOPING POLICY

Rules, regulations and policies are not new to the educational system; some are common sense, some evolve, some are mandated. There are different types for different situations.

In the last decade, both the Drug-Free Schools and Communities Act (DFSCA) and Drug-Free Workplace Act stimulated school districts to develop school drug policy. In 1988, the federal government required states to collect assurances from school districts receiving Drug-Free Schools funding that the districts had promulgated and implemented a policy on alcohol and other drugs. (The regulations did not request proof of implementation, just certification that a policy existed.)

Districts worked quickly to meet this DFSCA mandate. Sometimes an administrator wrote the policy. Some districts copied or purchased model policies from various sources. Still others spent considerable time developing and refining their own comprehensive document. While some of these policies were archived and forgotten, others were implemented, evaluated and modified to fit the district's needs.

The DFSCA reauthorization (as part of the Elementary and Secondary Education Act's (ESEA) amendment, known as "Improving America's School Act") has removed the original policy requirement. However, school districts all over the country continue to use school drug policy as part of an overall health and wellness strategy.

Policy matters can be complicated, so some schools have opted to duplicate another district's documents or reprint a model policy. While it is possible to use "boilerplate" templates, this approach is not recommended because a boilerplate:

1. Abrogates the desirable processes of learning, sharing and community-building.

2. Discounts stakeholders' input and expertise.

3. May not represent or reflect the needs and values of the community.

4. May not work as well as a policy developed specifically by and for the district.

Additionally, policies rushed into use cannot be expected to perform as well as a cohesive, comprehensive policy. The investment of time and effort in creating a custom-tailored document will be rewarded by a quality product that will serve students, families, the school and the community.

This chapter outlines the necessary steps for developing or revising policy.

LEADERSHIP

Due to legal, ethical and educational ramifications, policy projects must be handled in a highly professionally manner. For optimal success in policymaking, the project must have not only the support of the superintendent and central office administration but potent leadership as well.

Competent leadership will expedite the district's work, so the selection of a committee chair is an important task. Many districts appoint an administrator to oversee the policy process, although the committee chairperson may be a volunteer or be elected if the committee prefers. Many times two people will co-chair the group.

Chairpersons need to be well organized, and have the time, resources and skills to coordinate the committee's efforts. They need to work well with a group and interface with the committee and school.

STEPS TO POLICY DEVELOPMENT

1. Involve the School Attorney

Before initiating any policy work, involve the school attorney. Ask for a brief written outline of relevant federal and state laws, legal issues, decisions and guidelines that may pertain to the project. When possible, work actively with the district's attorney throughout the process. Provide a draft time line and ask for a review of the document prior to Board adoption.

2. Convene the Policy Committee

Policy development is most successful and effective when approached as a team process. A well-rounded team will yield a high-quality product with broad-based support. Invite a diverse group of participants to work on developing a policy that will be responsive to the needs of the school and the community.

Local needs, resources and interests will dictate the size of the policy team. An optimal team should include the following stake-holders:

- students (at least two)
- parents (at least two)
- administrator(s)
- building principal (at least one)
- member of district Board of Education
- special educator
- athletic director or coach
- staff organization or labor union representative
- health educator/coordinator
- student assistance counselor/school counselor
- health services professional/school nurse
- mental health professional
- clergy/faith community
- law enforcement/judicial representative
- local government official
- business/industry representative
- local drug/alcohol agency
- media representative

Invite participation by letter and follow up with a personal telephone call. The invitation can go to an agency or specific individual, as appropriate. This letter should identify the committee's purpose, its importance to the school and community, projected length of the project and the time and place of the initial committee meeting. Acknowledge the importance of wide representation on the committee. When possible, the superintendent or assistant superintendent and school board president should sign the letter. This demonstrates a high level of interest and commitment to prospective committee members. Include a date for reply, a telephone number and response card to be mailed or faxed back. Call those who have not responded by the deadline. For more efficient communication, collect phone numbers, fax numbers and e-mail addresses.

For optimum attendance at the first meeting, call committee members a day before the meeting to remind them of the time and place.

3. Orientation

The policy committee needs an introduction and an outline of the group's mission. At the initial meeting, explain the design and scope of the project, and review the purposes and benefits of policy (see Chapter 1).

Prepare a notebook for each committee member. The notebook should contain relevant documents, such as current policies and regulations, summaries of state and federal statutes, local ATOD statistics (if available) and emergency medical procedures. Include lined paper or a pad for participants to make notes and comments. When a schedule of meeting dates is ready, it can be inserted into the notebook for easy access.

At the first committee meeting, begin with the basics. After introductions, invite members, in their own words, to summarize what they know about the school's drug policy. Ask who has been involved in a policy-related case? (Remind the committee not to mention names.) What worked well and what needs to be changed?

Role play some or all of the case studies in Appendix D to stimulate creative thinking and highlight specific elements for discussion. This may take time, and be a challenge to convince committee members to act out roles. However, these role plays will yield valuable insights into weak, ambiguous, outdated or inappropriate elements that need to be revised. While it may seem convenient to omit this step, in the long run, using the case studies will prove to be a wise strategy.

Also arrange for a health educator or prevention professional to deliver a brief overview of ATOD prevention and how schools and communities can work together effectively.

4. Assess Local Needs

Needs assessment is a critical, but often overlooked, step. It is important to understand patterns and trends, attitudes and values concerning substance use and abuse within the school and community so that they can be addressed adequately in policy implementation and procedures. Data collection and documentation should drive policy, procedures and ongoing monitoring efforts. This information also helps make the case for local needs if challenges arise.

Information collection need not be overwhelming or expensive, and it should be done periodically. Student surveys, such as those developed by the University of Michigan, PRIDE or the Johnson Institute, can provide much more than simple statistics on drug abuse. (See Appendix E for a list of surveys.) Careful interpretation and comparison of data collected over time can help in spotting trends and emerging issues of immediate importance, as well as in providing other means of evaluating prevention programs and activities. Preserve all data, without identifying names, for any policy challenges in later years.

As an example, the Parents Resource Institute for Drug Education (PRIDE) has been polling American students about substance abuse for more than 20 years. Analysis of its national and local data reveals that school is the site where students are *least likely* to abuse drugs. The one exception to the pattern is inhalant abuse. Generally speaking, students reveal that abuse of inhalants is equally likely to occur at school as at other locations. Inhalant abuse is most common among middle school students and has been on the rise for more than a decade. Yet the problem is still relatively unknown among school staff. **Implications for policy:** specifically include inhalant chemicals and paraphernalia, and provide training for school personnel to raise awareness and provide the skills to recognize inhalant abuse.

Get a comprehensive picture of the ATOD trends in your area by using "key informant" interviews. Select seven or eight people for brief informational interviews using a question-and-answer format. Consider the following people as interviewees:

• chief of police	• custodial staff
• PTA/PTO president	• crisis/suicide hotline sponsor
• emergency room staff	
• poison control center staff	• Boys Club/Girls Club
	• youth bureau/youth worker(s)
• drug treatment center director	
	• juvenile justice staff
• department of health director	• probation officer
	• child protective services
• DWI coordinator	
	• family court judge
• housing authority supervisor	• mall/shopping center security
• recreation director	
	• clinic administrator
• school nurse	• school security supervisor

The ideal key informant interview will take less than 15 minutes. Prepare no more than four relevant questions and take notes during the discussion. Be sure to remind the informant not to use specific names. If names are mentioned, do not record them, as this may violate FERPA regulations.

Sample Questions:

- In the last 12 months, which substances are you seeing/discussing/treating most often in school-age youth?
- Which major issues related to ATOD did you see this year?

- Which behaviors/cases are you seeing recently that may be linked to alcohol and other abused drugs?

- Where are the most troublesome sites in your area and what is happening there?

- Are there any changes in youth drug issues that stand out in your mind?

- How are alcohol and other drugs involved in criminal behavior of local youth?

- Is there anything unusual or surprising in patterns of abuse that the school should know?

- What actions do you think the school should take?

Compile the key informant summaries into a single document for analysis and ease of reference, and disseminate to the policy committee.

These profiles of local drug abuse patterns can help the district allocate its resources wisely. Some districts use these data to make decisions about curricula, training, counseling or special programs.

Beyond internal use, release information to the public because it can be used to inform and rally the community. People are known to spring into action when they learn more about the problems of youth and drugs. Releasing survey data can help build support for prevention and intervention programs from parents, government, business and the community.

Anticipate and prepare for criticism or questions when the information is released, and the media is involved. Be sure to focus attention on the community, not just the school. Depending on the data, (1) print and broadcast media may run stories and request interviews, (2) current leaders may be criticized or take credit, (3) vendors may seize this opportunity to sell items, such as home drug tests, or (4) real estate agents may use the data when marketing to potential home buyers. Prepare clear charts and summary statements to clarify local data and to assure accuracy in reporting. Often the organization that distributes student drug surveys can help in preparing for public dissemination.

5. Assemble and Assess Documents

Most schools already have some statements or policies regarding substance abuse. Administrators and the school board clerk should carefully search active and archived documents to assemble all relevant materials, including policies, procedures and board attorney communications.

For instance, when the federal government adopted the Goals 2000 Act, smoking in schools and child care facilities was prohibited. To align with the new federal requirements, many school districts adopted a board policy prohibiting smoking in school buildings.

Think broadly to discover documents that might be overlooked. Check for related issues, such as state or district guidelines on medicine in school, emergency medical procedures, and intoxicated adults on school grounds.

Include relevant federal and state legislation, such as the Gun-Free Schools Act of 1994, Pro-Children's Act of 1994, Safe and Drug-Free Schools (latest amendments) as well as pertinent local statutes.

Contact your state department of education and state school boards association to request state regulations, sample policies and guidelines. Add any materials provided by the school attorney (unless confidential) to the collection of documents.

All relevant documents and materials should be photocopied and organized in a 3-ring binder for the use of each committee member. Where possible, the information can be provided on a computer disk or the Internet.

Review each policy document for accuracy, effectiveness and consistency. Search for descriptive explanations, not just simple yes/no items. Some questions to consider when assessing current policies include the following:

- Do the policies reflect current federal and state laws, and local ordinances?

- Are current policies consistent with the school's mission and philosophy?

- Are current policies easily accessible to the public?

- Are current policies clearly written and understandable to students, staff and community members?

- Have policies been widely disseminated and promoted?
- Are current policies enforceable as written?
- Are implementation and enforcement consistent?
- How are stakeholders' needs and concerns addressed?
- Do current policies address students, staff and other individuals?
- Do current policies cover a full range of sites and circumstances?
- Are staff roles and responsibilities clearly defined in current policies?
- Are accountability and record-keeping currently addressed?

6. Identify and Secure Resources

This project will take time and energy, and require a modest outlay of funds. Establish a budget for postage, photocopying, clerical support, telephoning, faxing and other basic services, in addition to beverages and light snacks for meetings. Also consider consultation expenses.

Safe and Drug-Free Schools Act (SDFSCA) monies can be used to pay for policy-related expenses. Alternatively, a district may elect to use general funds, seek a grant or request financial support from businesses or community organizations.

7. Establish a Time Line

How long will the process take? The time line will depend on the scope and nature of each project. Developing totally new policies and procedures takes more time than updates and revisions to existing documents. To produce quality work, establish the timetable as a guide and be prepared to adjust as needed.

In developing a time line, break the project down into components. Be sure to: (1) consider the size and nature of each task, (2) number of committee members, (3) estimate task and processing time for participants at meetings and outside of school hours,

(4) factor in expert input, clerical requirements and communication time, and (5) allow time for administrative procedures and review by experts, such as the school attorney.

A Gantt chart is a good format to use. The following is an example of a Gantt chart developed for a policy project initiated at the start of the school year.

TASK	Who's Responsible?	Due By
Assemble documents		October 1
Contact school attorney		October 15
Review and assess current policies		December 1
Conduct, analyze needs assessment		December 1
Determine scope of project, assign tasks		January 2
Plan for dissemination and implementation		January 2
Subcommittees complete duties		March 15
Schedule, chair interim meetings		as needed
Assemble, examine, revise materials		April 15
Supervise document preparation		May 1
Submit to school attorney		May 15
Revise if needed		June 10
Prepare for board approval		June 15
Staff training		August 15
Print, publicize, distribute		September 1
Evaluation, monitoring, training, update		annually or as needed

Determine which members will be responsible for which functions and distribute the completed form to all committee members.

8. School Board Approval/Adoption

The school board approves and officially adopts policies pertaining to students and staff. Requirements for board approval vary. The board clerk can advise about procedural and technical requirements, including agenda schedules and due dates. Committees should format documents accordingly and provide the appropriate number of originals and copies for the board.

The policy-making committee should take time to prepare for its presentation to the board. Select an appropriate spokesperson, one who has thorough knowledge of the development and writing process and who can answer questions or discuss specific issues raised by Board Members.

CHECKLIST	Date Completed
❏ Leadership and support	_____
❏ Involve school attorney	_____
❏ Assemble and orient stakeholder team	_____
❏ Needs assessment	_____
❏ Collect, assess relevant documents	_____
❏ Estimate resources	_____
❏ Develop time line	_____
❏ Distribute tasks	_____
❏ Prepare for Board approval	_____

Chapter 3

ESSENTIAL COMPONENTS OF SCHOOL DRUG POLICY

Drug prevention begins with education, a point congruent with the educational mission of schools. A comprehensive school policy will complement the educational process, promote discipline and school safety, frame the scope of the issues involved, and clearly describe relevant goals, elements and resources.

Because of the visibility of ATOD issues and the legal, financial and ethical concerns involved in policies, it is in the school's best interest to take the time to craft a clear and cohesive policy document. This chapter outlines the elements to include in a comprehensive school drug policy.

INTRODUCTION: RATIONALE AND PHILOSOPHY

This brief section should delineate the reasons for creating and implementing a school drug policy. The opening paragraph may be a simple declaration of recognition and concern about ATOD issues and can be followed by a statement of support for Goal 7 of the "Goals for the Nation 2000":

> *Every school in the United States will be free of drugs, violence, and the unauthorized presence of firearms and alcohol, and will offer a disciplined environment conducive to learning.*

Include the district's mission statement, with an explanation of how the drug policy relates to the school's mission and to the health and safety of students and employees. A statement acknowledging the importance of the district's pro-active role in education, prevention, and early intervention efforts may be augmented by a concluding paragraph that summarizes the policy development process.

GENERAL STATEMENT OF SCHOOL POLICY ON ATOD

A general statement of purpose sets the parameters for the school's policy and generally identifies the basics—who, what, where, when, how—pertinent to the policy.

Some districts define the "who" by listing groups of people, such as students and staff. However, this definition can certainly be broader and more general. The "what" must be as inclusive and specific as possible to serve notice that any and all ATOD-related activities are prohibited. In terms of "where," the policy can cover the most territory by referring to school property, buildings and grounds, school-sponsored transportation, and off-site events. Federal, state and local statutes may allow language that describes "drug-free school zones" within a specified distance from the school's property lines.

Defining the "when" becomes a challenge. If the policy indicates "school hours" or "at school," then some may interpret that as allowing ATOD abuse after school hours. Because many students participate in school-sponsored events, such as weekend athletic events, and field trips, it is important to be as inclusive and specific as possible. One way to bridge this gap is to connect the "when" with the "where" so that it is clear that ATOD-related behaviors are prohibited and will not be tolerated on school property *or* at school-sponsored events at other sites.

Identify classes of prohibited and controlled substances to illustrate the policy's intent and extent. This should include illicit drug categories as well as over-the-counter and prescription medicines. How much to include? The level of detail is a matter of choice, but it is better to err on the side of too much rather than too little. Your school attorney can provide appropriate statutory language to include controlled substances defined by state penal, drug and juvenile codes. The list can be seen as a demonstration of the district's level of awareness, while serving notice to potential violators. It should be clear that this is a partial list, that is not meant to be all-inclusive.

The following statement, adapted from *A Framework for Prevention: A Guide for Developing a Comprehensive School Policy Concerning Alcohol and Other Substances* by the New York State Education Department, can be used as a model.

> *No person may possess, use, produce, sell or distribute alcohol or other substances, nor use or possess paraphernalia for the purpose of drug use, at any time, in school buildings, on school property and grounds, in school-sponsored vehicles or at school-sponsored events at other sites. The terms "alcohol, drugs and other substances" shall be construed to refer to all substances in all forms, including, but not limited to: alcohol and alcohol-containing beverages; all forms of tobacco; inhalable substances (such as gases, solvents, butane, propane, adhesives); marijuana or its derivatives; cocaine/crack; LSD or other hallucinogenic drugs; PCP; amphetamines and amphetamine-like compounds; heroin; methadone; scheduled narcotics; steroids; herbal/"natural" stimulants, herbal/ "natural" euphoriants; look-alike products; and any substances commonly referred to as "designer drugs." The inappropriate and/or illegal use of prescription and over-the-counter preparations is prohibited. Prescription medication or over-the-counter preparations for personal use shall be allowed only as per district medication policy, under the supervision of school personnel, with written orders from a physician. Federal, state and local laws shall apply to students and employees alike.*

STUDENTS AND EMPLOYEES

It is necessary to address ATOD issues for both students and adults (e.g., employees, volunteers), either in separate documents or combined into a single policy, as both groups are school-based. In addition, districts that receive federal grants may be subject to the Drug-Free Workplace Act, which requires a written policy on substance abuse.

The employee policy must be well organized, disseminated, monitored and evaluated. Consult Appendix E for resources that can provide technical assistance for employee workplace drug policies.

SCHOOL HEALTH EDUCATION

The most successful prevention efforts include ATOD prevention as a component of a coordinated school health education (CSHE) program. The CSHE model, as defined by the American School Health Association and the Centers for Disease Control and Prevention, includes eight components:

1. healthful school environment

2. health instruction

3. health services

4. physical education

5. guidance and counseling services

6. food service

7. school-site wellness

8. integrated school/community programs

Each component is important in facilitating student health and wellness. ATOD prevention can be addressed as an integral part of each component. For example, consider the following: (1) how tobacco use in bathrooms impacts the school environment, (2) ethical issues of athletes and steroids, and (3) drug-free community activities hosted at the school.

Policy and prevention issues integrate well with most K-12 instructional programs and the CSHE program. Concerning health instruction, the Division for Adolescent and School Health unit of the Centers for Disease Control and Prevention developed the following definition of health education:

Health Education is a planned, sequential, K-12 curriculum that addresses the physical, mental, emotional and social dimensions of health. The curriculum is designed to motivate and assist students to maintain and improve their health-related risk behaviors. It allows students to develop and demonstrate increasingly sophisticated health-related knowledge, attitudes, skills and practices. The curriculum is comprehensive and includes a variety of topics such as personal health, family health, community health, consumer health, environmental

*health, family life, mental and emotional health, injury preven-
tion and safety, nutrition, prevention and control of disease, and
substance use and abuse.*

Each health curriculum topic may include dimensions related
to ATOD prevention, just as a quality instructional program will
highlight and clarify ATOD issues, connecting them to health education and, thereby, strengthening the districtwide prevention
plan.

PREVENTION

Three decades of prevention research provide guiding principles
for effective ATOD prevention. A comprehensive policy document briefly describes how the district addresses each research-
validated ATOD prevention principle in the following ways:

1. *Accurate, current, age-appropriate information through credi-
   ble sources.*

   A one-paragraph description of the district's latest curriculum and training efforts related to ATOD. If a district
   has invested in a specific curriculum, mention it by name
   and grade level. If applicable, include a sentence affirm-
   ing the district's commitment to ongoing training and
   awareness to keep staff abreast of current issues and
   trends.

2. *Enhancement of social and life skills.*

   One or two sentences to describe existing programs for
   developing, practicing or enhancing social and life skills.

3. *Peers as resources.*

   Research reveals that peer influence is powerful. List district programs, such as peer helpers, peer leaders, peer
   tutoring and peer mentors.

4. *Positive alternatives.*

   Schools afford multiple opportunities for students to
   become involved in drug-free activities. Acknowledge
   these in the form of a statement of support and recognition of clubs and sports teams.

5. *Early identification of individuals at risk.*

   Because students spend so much time in the school set-ting, school personnel are in an excellent position to iden-tify possible problems and intervene. A simple statement of purpose, intent and process will acknowledge the roles of student assistance counselors, guidance counselors, school nurse, social workers and school psychologist.

6. *Prevention counseling and intervention, and referral services.*

   Student assistance counselors or other trained profession-als often provide assessment, referral and counseling ser-vices to students in school. Include a section identifying specialized professionals working in this area or delineate how the school works with "high-risk" students. Include mechanisms for referral to community-based agencies and services.

The Department of Education Safe and Drug-Free Schools Program recently published its *Principles of Effectiveness* to govern use of resources under the Safe and Drug-Free Schools Act (DFSCA.) See Appendix C for the complete document. These prin-ciples state that the recipient of SDFSCA funding shall:

- Base its programs on a thorough assessment of objective data about the drug and violence problems in the schools and communities served.

- With the assistance of a local or regional advisory council where required by the SDFSCA, establish a set of measur-able goals and objectives and design its programs to meet those goals and objectives.

- Design and implement its programs for youth based on research or evaluation that provides evidence that the programs used prevent or reduce drug use, violence, or disruptive behavior among youth.

- Evaluate its programs periodically to assess its progress toward achieving its goals and objectives, and use its evaluation results to refine, improve, and strengthen its program, while refining its goals and objectives as appro-priate.

INTERVENTION, AFTER-CARE AND RE-ENTRY

Intervention is often triggered by a policy infraction. And, indeed, identification of individuals involved in or affected by ATOD abuse should lead to intervention. Mechanisms of intervention can include in-school and outside of school ATOD assessment, referral, parent meeting and support groups. In-school intervention processes can be mentioned in this section of the policy, such as students voluntarily seeking assistance, core team referral, staff referral measures and peer concern referrals. Confidentiality should be acknowledged as a valid concern and the district's Family Educational Rights and Privacy Act (FERPA) policy or other federal/state confidentiality regulations may be affirmed in this section. Specific confidentiality guidelines, if available, also can be included. However, reserve detailed intervention procedures for inclusion in district procedures for policy implementation.

It is vital to support students who are in treatment or returning from treatment, to achieve success. Some student assistance programs run support groups for re-entering students and also help them to access services. These students may have missed instructional time and may require tutoring or extra help. They also may need flexibility in their daily schedules to catch up. Students with ATOD problems can benefit from school-based support groups and a positive relationship with a concerned adult. The policy can reflect these goals. Again, simple statements will suffice in the policy; detailed procedures belong in separate implementation documents.

RESOURCES/EMPLOYEE ASSISTANCE PROGRAM

Both students and employees need to know how to deal with ATOD-related problems, questions and concerns. In many cases, students can visit with a student assistance counselor to request information. To provide the most information to the most people, compile, publish and post a list of in-school and community-based resources. Several times a year publish local or national "hotline" numbers in the school newspaper. Use bulletin boards to promote agencies and organizations. Information can be made available in the office of the building administrator, school nurse, guidance counselor, school psychologist or social worker.

Resources are an important issue for employees. One in 12 full-time employees reports current usage of an illicit drug (National Institute for Drug Abuse, 1996). Consider the implications of substance-abusing workers: They are more likely to sustain injuries, miss work, report illness or be late. They may not perform satisfactorily, or they may interfere with others' work. Employees are an investment; therefore, it is imperative to offer employees access to help and services. A confidential interview, assessment and referral can be most effective in reducing stigma, embarrassment or fear of reprisal. Employee Assistance Programs (EAP) bring information and resources to those in need, either for themselves or their families. It is important to mention the EAP in this section of the staff policy document.

If the district does not provide an EAP, it is most advisable to compile a current list of resources that employees might need and update it annually. Refer to this resource list in the policy or place it within the policy. In the interest of providing resources and assistance to employees, this list should be updated and distributed regularly. An annual cycle is highly recommended.

This list could include the employee health benefits administrator; state and local government agencies, such as County Mental Health Services; community-based agencies, such as local affiliates of the National Council on Alcoholism and Drug Dependence; smoking cessation service providers, such as the American Cancer Society or American Lung Association; substance abuse treatment providers; self-help resources like Alcoholics Anonymous, Al-Anon and other 12-step programs; local hospitals or clinics; and national clearinghouses, such as the National Clearinghouse for Alcohol and Drug Information (NCADI). Check with the district's health insurance providers and include their resources. Make sure that employees understand their benefits.

DISCIPLINARY MEASURES/CODES OF CONDUCT

School drug policy must be augmented by defined, written codes of conduct. These may be labeled discipline code, behavior policy, rules of conduct, code of conduct or disciplinary policy. No matter what the label, the code of conduct generally refers to the behavioral standards and expectations of the school community.

It is imperative that the code be formalized, put in writing and widely disseminated. Just as with the school drug policy, advance notice and clear parameters can go a long way toward setting the tone for behavior. Written discipline codes can help assure fair and consistent management.

The code of conduct outlines behavioral expectations and identifies violations along with sanctions for infractions. Many codes phrase behavioral expectations in a positive manner. For instance, a code may state, "School District ABC encourages and promotes student conduct that demonstrates respect for self and others, and fosters a positive learning climate." In general, these codes will subsequently identify specific violations and the consequences, including any escalation in consequences for subsequent violations. For example, the code may prohibit fighting, hitting, kicking, biting or other physical means of assault and proscribe a three-day suspension for the first offense, a five-day suspension for the second offense and a 10-day suspension for the third offense. In addition, the code may list other conditions, such as referral to the school guidance counselor, referral to the conflict mediation program, and the principal's hearing with parent and student.

It will not be possible to foresee every situation that may occur. Select representative violations by researching past experiences and formalize the school's response to each violation. Local juvenile authorities can help with sample offenses and appropriate policy language. There may be four or five specific issues listed, along with the consequences for each. Flexibility is a double-edged sword, so consider carefully what is and is not written, especially the legal implications of not having a written code of conduct. A written code is preferable, so be sure that the policy's language clearly states that this list is not intended to be totally inclusive. Check through the written codes annually and keep complete documentation of all cases.

ACCOUNTABILITY

As policies and procedures are developed, it is wise to build in checks and balances for accountability purposes. Clarify roles and responsibilities, in writing, and make sure that all staff members understand how their participation enhances the success of the school's policy. Check with the school attorney about the use of an annual sign-off sheet to indicate that each district employee has read and will comply with the school's drug policy. Some districts make this part of the opening-day schedule, following a brief policy review session for returning employees.

Staff, administrators and supervisors should be mindful of their accountability to the superintendent, school board and community. Make certain their supervisory duties are spelled out in detail and that individuals are prepared for these roles. Should policy or procedures be questioned, a district must be prepared to document the acts of its employees. Staff members who document and report concerns must be assured that supervisors will consistently follow through and intervene according to the policy and the law.

STAFF DEVELOPMENT

A comprehensive policy should acknowledge the district's support and commitment to ongoing staff development. This may include a general statement that promotes the need for training and the district's intent to sponsor training opportunities and information dissemination on an ongoing basis.

The success of the overall prevention program relies on a staff that is informed, prepared and able and willing to assume positive roles in relation to young people. Therefore, additional training opportunities must be provided regularly. Many districts provide training in specific prevention programs or curricula and augment this with other workshops. Prevention-related topics may include the following:

- principles of prevention
- primer on drug trends or specific drugs
- building self-esteem
- enhancing student resiliency
- understanding alcoholism and alcoholic family systems
- primer on addiction(s)

- helping a young person or a friend who has a problem with alcohol or other drugs and smoking cessation

CHECKLIST	Date Completed
☐ Introduction/philosophy, stressing awareness and values	_____
☐ General policy statement: who, what, where, when, why	_____
☐ Address both students and employees	_____
☐ Prevention linked to coordinated school health education	_____
☐ Prevention programs/activities outlined	_____
☐ Intervention, after-care/re-entry services	_____
☐ Resources/employee assistance program	_____
☐ Discipline/conduct code	_____
☐ Accountability	_____
☐ Staff development	_____

Chapter 4

PROCEDURES FOR IMPLEMENTATION AND ENFORCEMENT

Even the best policies are destined to fail if they are either poorly or never implemented. Policies require procedures to guide operations. Planning for implementation should begin at the same time as policy development or the revision process begins. This chapter outlines suggestions for implementation procedures.

IMPLEMENTATION TRAINING

As described in Chapter 2, all staff members need information and guidance on policy implementation, enforcement, roles/responsibilities, etc., because staff should be prepared to act appropriately if the need arises. For instance, if the school secretary is collecting papers from a student and notices a strong odor of alcohol on the student's breath, the secretary needs to know who to notify and exactly what to do. Procedures should specify what is to be done, by whom and in which order. Training must clarify procedures so that everyone can support and enforce policies.

Training should not be considered a single event, but rather part of an overall management plan. It should be an ongoing process. Provide in-depth training initially and reinforce the training with reminders built into staff meetings and other events.

ROLES AND RESPONSIBILITIES

Who has responsibility for policy implantation and enforcement? For policies to be effective, everyone must participate. Written procedures make staff roles clear and manageable by indicating a chain of command and prescribed courses of action to be taken.

31

Standardized forms and guidelines for documentation are vital, and procedures should detail how situations are to be handled. In multibuilding school districts, provision should be made for a supervisory contact person in each building. Generally the principal or top building administrator serves this role. A designee should also be named in the event the administrator is not available.

Some school policies require that the school nurse, if available, interview a student under suspicion of alcohol or other drug use. What does this mean in actual practice? What are the limitations of this expectation? What legal issues, such as licensure or professional practice, might be involved? The school's attorney can do research and advise on this matter. All procedures must be clarified for referral.

Who must be present? What questions may be asked? What signs or symptoms should be checked, recorded or reported? To whom should the report be made? What is kept in confidence, and what is reported to parents? Who is to be notified, and who will do the notification? A written summary of procedures that addresses these questions should be disseminated to all personnel who might be involved.

PILOT-TEST AND REFINEMENT PROCEDURES

Do not minimize or shortcut the development of specific procedures; they are critical to successful policy implementation. Use the sample scenarios and plan procedural steps carefully. Test implementation by role playing several case studies from beginning to end. (See case studies in Appendix D.)

Assign roles, appoint two people to record events, and play out possible scenarios involving school drug policy. This will help identify gaps in the policy and pinpoint inconsistencies or reveal vague directions. Use the experiences of the recorders and role-playing staff to help clarify procedures and prepare for training.

COOPERATION WITH LAW ENFORCEMENT AGENCIES

Keep in mind the need to establish and maintain a working relationship with local law enforcement officials before an incident occurs. School administrators need to know which circumstances necessitate police involvement. With the assistance of these officials, formalize a list of violations or incidents that would necessitate the involvement of law enforcement. These will most probably include infractions of law, such as the sale or possession of a controlled substance or felony-level possession of substances, but they also may include other specific cases and incidents worth noting. This information must be part of policy-related training so that staff members will know when law enforcement must become involved.

FAIR AND CONSISTENT ENFORCEMENT

All people must be treated equally in the application or enforcement of policy. This principle is critical to the success of school policy and prevention programs, as it signals the school district's desire that all students and staff be healthy and drug-free. Fair and consistent enforcement districtwide will be supported by staff, students, parents and community members alike. It also can forestall litigation or claims based on preferential treatment or selective enforcement.

In practice, this means that all cases should be treated alike. If, for example, the study hall supervisor refers student A to the principal under suspicion of drug use, under the same circumstances student B must be referred the same way. The fact that student B is the basketball team's star forward (or Honor Society member or child of an influential politician) should not and *cannot* influence the enforcement of policy. Similarly, if student B is allowed to make up work missed during a policy-related suspension, then student A must have the same privilege. This is not only common sense but a responsible, legally defensible way for schools to operate.

Does this affect an administrator's decision-making authority? Perhaps. However desirable flexibility is in many educational arenas, too much flexibility can be detrimental to the success of a school's discipline or drug policies, especially if it appears that "some are more equal than others." Too much flexibility may make policy unclear or unenforceable and could result in charges of unfairness or potential litigation.

The importance of adhering to the spirit of fair and consistent enforcement cannot be overstated. Children, young people and adults tend to respond favorably in support of policies they perceive to be fair and equitable. Any hint of favoritism or discriminatory action could jeopardize both the policy and the ultimate goal of a safe and drug-free school. Build in an appeals process to enhance objectivity and consistency, with another administrator as reviewer. Remind personnel of their responsibility to be consistent and fair in their policy-related duties.

MONITORING

How will the district know that policy and procedures are working? A process for monitoring can provide information, feedback and support and should be established when the policy is written or revised.

There is no substitute for board interest and support, so consider an annual report to the school board. If the board demands more than a "pro forma" report and expects to hear comments from a cross section of stakeholders, this can provide the impetus for serious solicitation of feedback and widespread understanding and support for school drug policy.

Be sure to build in a process for students, staff, community members and parents who want input or wish to discuss changes. Policies with the broadest base of support are the most successful. A culture of inclusion helps to make stakeholders part of the process and part of the solution.

There are many ways to do this. The DAC could provide an appropriate forum, with policy/procedures as an agenda item. Or the assistant superintendent for pupil personnel could convene a meeting or solicit comments once a year. Building-level governance/shared decision-making committees may be helpful in gathering information, as can parent-teacher organizations. The school newsletter and Web site can carry policy information, with an address or telephone number to encourage feedback. A student Key Club, Future Business Leaders of America club, Youth Bureau, Students Against Destructive Decisions (SADD) or other student group can conduct informal surveys or sponsor a "speak up" forum to encourage student participation.

REVIEW, MODIFICATION AND UPDATING

Revisit policies and procedures regularly to keep them current, legal, responsive, and enforceable. Generally, policy review should take place once a year.

Prior to the full review, consult the school attorney for relevant case law or legislative changes that should be incorporated. Drug trends change rapidly. Therefore review policy for more complete inclusion of substances and paraphernalia. Discuss reports of gang and criminal activities with local law enforcement agencies. Ask the school attorney to keep track of state or federal regulation changes that would require a policy update. Consult with special education supervisors and school health specialists about medication issues that may need to be addressed. Also, be sure to query counselors and health services staff.

To keep policy and procedures current and defensible, use the feedback from your monitoring efforts and solicit additional comments from staff, particularly those who have been directly involved in implementing or monitoring efforts.

	Date
CHECKLIST	**Completed**

☐ Clearly define roles, responsibilities
and procedures   _____

☐ Provide adequate and regular training
and policy review   _____

☐ Pilot and refine procedures   _____

☐ Insist on fair, consistent enforcement   _____

☐ Build in accountability   _____

☐ Require signatures to indicate staff
members have received policy   _____

☐ Plan to monitor policy implementation
and effectiveness   _____

☐ Review policies and procedures regularly   _____

☐ Update as needed or when required by
law   _____

Chapter 5

DISSEMINATING, PUBLICIZING AND PROMOTING POLICY

Once policies and regulations have been board-approved and procedures are in place, it is time to "get the word out." This critical stage cannot be overlooked or short-circuited. By disseminating policies, the district is publicly announcing acceptable standards of conduct. Educating students, staff and the community about district policy provides an excellent forum for promoting drug-free values, and confirms the school/community partnership. A widely publicized policy demonstrates the school's continuing commitment to working with families and the community.

Promotion should take place on many levels. Before initiating a widespread publicity campaign, start within the district, making sure there are sufficient written copies of all documents.

BEGIN WITH STAFF

Policymakers can meet with district-level and building-level administrators and staff-organization representatives to brief them on the policy. People who have been part of the development process will be particularly helpful in answering questions and helping others understand their roles and responsibilities. Allow sufficient time for questions and exploration of procedural issues to ensure that key personnel are prepared for policy implementation.

The goal of a drug-free school requires active participation from all employees. Remember to include librarians, hall monitors, security guards, bus drivers, cafeteria workers, custodians, coaches, health services personnel, counselors, social workers, clerical and secretarial support staff—literally everyone who is associated with the school district.

Inform all parties about the new policies and procedures in writing, but do not rely solely on written notice. The policy should be included in the district's personnel manual or employment contract. Make sure that all the information is also discussed orally, preferably in meetings where people can interact. Communicate in as personal a manner as possible so that employees feel supported during the implementation process. Consider using a case study to role play as a model for staff. Also invite people to play roles in other scenarios. This increases the comfort level and introduces questions that need clarification or review, assuring more consistent implementation.

INFORMING COMMUNITY AGENCIES

Be sure to inform community agencies about the new policies and procedures. A written summary and oral discussion will suffice. Do not forget health-related staff, social workers or counselors who may be employed by outside organizations. These agencies are expected to support drug policy implementation but may have special confidentiality issues that must be addressed.

INFORMING STUDENTS

School drug policies help protect students and make school a safe place for all. Students must be informed of the policy's overall goals and tenets, as well as be assured of their rights and responsibilities.

Who will introduce the policies to students? How and when will it be done? Plan your activities carefully and remain consistent, for this will set the tone for understanding and acceptance. Students should receive a summary of the policy and the full policy should be readily available to all students, perhaps in a handbook that they and their parents can read. Many school districts require students and parents to sign a statement of receipt of discipline codes.

PUBLIC DISSEMINATION

Once staff and students are informed, plan for wider dissemination of your policy, starting with parents. Prepare a summary of the policy and relevant procedures and make sure that parents receive a copy. Some districts mail a policy summary to every family as part of their back-to-school mailing. The school calendar would also serve this purpose. Use parent meetings as an opportunity to promote the policies and ask for parental support and reinforcement.

The community should be kept informed, as well. This can be accomplished as follows:

Post an updated summary of policy:
- in every administrative office.
- on the school's Web site.
- at the main entrance to each school building.
- in the school store.
- in cafeterias for students and staff.

Annually, publish a summary in:
- parent newsletters.
- teacher's handbook.
- staff organization newsletter.
- student newspaper.
- student handbook/code of conduct.
- district calendar.
- athletic programs.
- yearbook.

As appropriate, attach a summary to:
- athlete's code of conduct.
- application for student parking permit.
- contracts of major vendors.
- special education committee information packet.

- school trip consent form.
- peer leadership application.
- ticket request for prom or other event.

On an annual basis:

- remind teachers to review policy with students and to reiterate their support for a safe and drug-free school.
- review policies and procedures at a faculty meeting or staff development day.
- broadcast public service announcements on local cable access channel or radio station.
- run the written policy summary on cable access channel.

CHECKLIST	Date Completed
❑ Ample copies of full policy and procedures, plus summaries	_____
❑ All staff receive copies of policy and procedures	_____
❑ Face-to-face discussion of policy with administrators, staff	_____
❑ Staff review policy highlights with students	_____
❑ Students receive policy or summary	_____
❑ Parents and community members informed of policy/signed acknowledgement	_____
❑ Publicize and promote policy	_____
❑ Policy is reviewed with staff and students annually and at other appropriate times	_____

Chapter 6

ISSUES FOR SPECIAL CONSIDERATION

DRUG TESTING: STUDENTS

Some school systems have turned to drug testing as another method of working toward a safe and drug-free school. Because of the legal issues involved, two populations will be considered: general student populations and student athletes.

Drug testing of the general student population falls under the Fourth Amendment to the Constitution, which prohibits unreasonable searches and seizures which, unless undertaken with exceptional care, may result in litigation against the district. For this reason, the decision to initiate a drug-testing program should only be made after extensive discussion and analysis, and should *never* occur without consulting the school attorney.

Limited random drug testing of students is being conducted under very controlled conditions in a few school systems. When following this course of action, schools need to address the following:

- consent of parent/guardian
- cost of testing
- selection of kits and laboratory (cost versus medical accuracy)
- specify drugs to be identified by test (cost versus medical accuracy)
- random selection of subjects
- test interval (e.g., monthly, quarterly)
- prior notice versus unannounced drug tests
- privacy versus observed specimen

- "chain of custody" to assure verifiable sample
- retest procedures
- notification procedures
- confidentiality of procedure and records
- intervention and referral procedures
- explicit consequences as a result of positive drug test

Students involved in athletics may now be subject to drug testing, per a 1995 U.S. Supreme Court decision, known as the Vernonia case. While the Court found it to be reasonable to drug test athletes, it also warned that drug testing of the general student body, except in a random manner, would not be considered reasonable. The Court decision inferred that athletes have a reduced expectation of privacy due to the nature of sports activities/locker room conditions and that because of their voluntary participation, they can be subject to more restrictive regulations than the general student body.

In light of this precedent, some school systems have already initiated drug testing programs for students involved in athletics and extracurricular activities, such as cheerleading, and other such voluntary student activities.

Drug testing has also been used in instances in which a school administrator has *reasonable cause* to suspect that a student is under the influence of alcohol or other drugs. Most procedures of this type require documentation of signs and symptoms of drug use. A drug test may be requested by the school nurse or other medical authority and must be authorized by a parent or guardian. Again, be cautious about initiating any drug testing protocol without consulting legal counsel. Policies, procedures and "reasonable cause" must be defined and determined by an attorney familiar with student drug testing issues.

DRUG TESTING: EMPLOYEES

Drug testing programs exist in many workplaces. Testing employees for drugs, however, will not reduce employee drug misuse and abuse. It is but a single element of a comprehensive prevention program. Public safety is a key concern in determining the legitimacy of drug testing of employees.

The decision to drug test employees should only be made after consulting with staff representatives and the school attorney. Legal counsel can investigate the impact of recent court decisions on the configuration of testing programs and research applicable federal, state and local laws. Transportation law has particular importance to those employees engaged in transporting students.

If the district's employee Code of Conduct calls for disciplinary action if a staff member is found to be under the influence of alcohol or other drugs, obtain a written legal opinion concerning ATOD abuse as a disabling condition and insert a summary into the code.

In addition to the issues identified for student drug testing, consider the following:

- Who will be tested (e.g., job applicants, new employees, administrators, bus drivers and mechanics)?

- Union or contractual issues.

DRUG POLICY FOR ATHLETES

Due to the nature of sports, athletes face the risk of injury while in training or during competition. Use of alcohol or other drugs increases the potential for injury to self and others. Most schools have a "Chemical Code of Conduct" for students in competitive sport that details their responsibilities to stay drug-free. These contracts often require an athlete to abstain from alcohol and other drugs during training and throughout the sports season. It is generally signed by athletes and their parents.

Be careful, though, as this contract could be interpreted incorrectly. Its emphasis on abstinence at specific times (during training and the sports season) might be viewed by students or parents as prohibiting ATOD use *only* during those times. A special contract for athletes could backfire, as some athletes may assume that the school's general drug policy does not apply to them!

Different policies for athletes and the general student population could open the door to legal challenge, based on inconsistent enforcement or discrimination against a class of people (athletes).

For these reasons, separate policies for athletes are not recommended. If desired, the school can reprint or excerpt the district's drug policy and use it as a contract for all extracurricular activities, including sports. This can be signed by students and parents and will serve as a reminder of how the school works to protect their health and safety. A policy summary can be reprinted in the game program as a means of informing students and spectators.

SEARCHING FOR DRUGS

In a continuing effort to maintain a safe and drug-free school, some districts are retaining control of specific property on their premises. Courts have agreed that, under certain conditions, school officials have the right to search locations, such as desks and lockers, without the express permission of the individual, whether student *or* employee, currently using them. Some court decisions have also upheld the school's right to inspect backpacks, handbags and similar items under specific circumstances. Cars parked on school property may also be subject to search. To avoid legal problems, consult with the school attorney before initiating or modifying a search policy.

It is important to provide written notice to students and staff that lockers, desks, closets, file cabinets, drawers and line equipment remain the property of the school district, even when in use by an individual and that this property may be inspected at any time by school officials. Some experts suggest that this policy be reviewed orally at least once a year in addition to providing annual written notice.

Although a few districts have also used drug-sniffing dogs, this method of search should be approached with caution. In general, individuals may not be "sniffed" without a search warrant, although school property, such as lockers, desks and vehicles can be checked by trained dogs. Competent legal advice can help to build defensible policies and procedures without undue liability.

PROTECTING AND PRESERVING
POTENTIAL EVIDENCE

Drugs, drug paraphernalia and suspicious substances *do* turn up in schools. Materials of this sort have been found in bathrooms, locker rooms, basement corners, schoolyards, parking lots and even on the roof. It is essential that schools develop good working relationships with local law enforcement agencies and officials, and work with these professionals in developing procedures for securing questionable materials.

For legal reasons, schools should plan carefully for this eventuality. Keep a record of the circumstances surrounding the event, including date, time and exact location where the material was taken into official possession. A school must establish a "chain of custody" that assures property will be secure and protected from the moment it comes into their possession until it is turned over to authorities.

Drug-related items found on school property or confiscated from students must be treated as potential evidence. As such, the discovery or confiscation must be well-documented and all physical evidence should be carefully protected from tampering or destruction. Seal the evidence in a bag or envelope and immediately label it with date, time, place and names of witnesses. Summon law enforcement officials as soon as possible.

Local law enforcement authorities can provide advice on appropriate "chain of custody" procedures. Once such procedures are in place, be sure to train staff in implementation.

Chapter 7

ASSEMBLING A DISTRICT
ADVISORY COUNCIL

BENEFITS OF AN ADVISORY COUNCIL

Advisory groups validate the community's interest in, and responsibility for, productive schools. Each member has the potential to contribute unique talents, knowledge, enthusiasm and skills that go a long way toward making a well-rounded working group.

Involving a cross-section of the community in school business builds active support for programs and policies. Their input can make the difference between acceptance, apathy or rejection of policies and procedures. Representing many diverse concerns, these people work on important issues, thus enhancing the credibility of the programs and the school. Advisory council members tend to generate favorable "word of mouth" support and often become champions for policies and programs.

Consider the hidden benefits of advisors and the resources they represent. A judge serving on your advisory group might speak at the D.A.R.E. graduation or offer assistance to the business law class. A parent with a background in health care administration may work with the school nurse to streamline office procedures. Welcoming the community into the school means gaining its enthusiasm and expertise and sharing the responsibilities in maintaining healthy students.

ADVISORY COUNCIL REQUIREMENTS UNDER ESEA
TITLE IV: SAFE AND DRUG-FREE SCHOOLS ACT

Schools receiving federal funds under ESEA Title IV, known as the Safe and Drug-Free Schools and Communities Act (SDFSCA), are required to convene a group of advisors, as spelled out in the legislation. [See Appendix A for legislation, Section 4115 (a) (2).]

The chief operating officers for schools receiving such grant funds generally sign a series of assurance statements in the grant application. Two of these merit particular attention: the clause requiring an advisory panel, and the Drug-Free Workplace Act. Information about the Drug-Free Workplace Act of 1988 can be found in Chapter 1 of this Guide.

DRUG ADVISORY COUNCIL AND THE SCHOOL'S HEALTH ADVISORY COUNCIL

Because of the dynamic nature of health education issues, schools continually need to review and update their curricula, materials, and teaching strategies. Some content areas present a challenge because they may be perceived as sensitive or controversial. For instance, many schools are required to convene advisory panels for HIV/AIDS curriculum issues and family life and sexuality education programs. These tasks (and others) need not necessitate the formation of yet another panel, but can be addressed efficiently and effectively through the activities of a districtwide school health advisory group, saving time and volunteers' energy.

As noted in Chapter 3 of this Guide, ATOD issues are most appropriately addressed in the context of Coordinated School Health Education. Therefore, many schools prefer to establish the DAC as a subcommittee of a larger umbrella group, the Health Advisory Council (HAC). This districtwide HAC deals with all health-related issues. Its members should be a diverse group. Schools that use a HAC designate subcommittees to deal with specific issues, such as ATOD or HIV/AIDS. These subcommittees meet as needed, complete their tasks and report back to the HAC. Individuals can be invited to participate on subcommittees at the pleasure of the HAC or subcommittee chair so that the group can remain at a workable number. Conducting business in this manner is efficient and effective and assures continuity. It also reduces the risk of burnout or overuse of key individuals.

GETTING STARTED/REVITALIZING THE DRUG ADVISORY COUNCIL

Whether this is a new undertaking or an attempt to resurrect a dormant committee, certain steps apply. Leadership is key! A board that selects a high-level district administrator to oversee the advisory council process broadcasts an implicit message of the significance of the group's work.

Once leadership is in place, commence (or resurrect) the districtwide DAC by sending out a call for members. Be prepared for questions about previous committee composition or work done in the past, but emphasize the need to start fresh and work on developing a strong, cohesive working group.

MEMBERSHIP CATEGORIES

ESEA Title IV, Section 4115 (a) (2) legislation defines the categories of individuals who should be represented on the districtwide Drug Advisory Council as:

- local government officials
- parents
- teachers
- appropriate state agencies
- medical professional
- community-based organizations

- business
- students
- pupil services personnel
- private schools
- law enforcement
- groups with interest/ expertise in drug and violence prevention

Within these designated categories, the district may use its discretion to invite specific individuals to join.

Local government officials includes officials of the town, city or county—a supervisor, board member, or director of a government department, such as the recreation department, or the official's designee.

Business includes a local business owner or representatives of businesses in the area. Many local banks, insurance agencies and other firms send employees to serve with schools, and the chamber of commerce may participate if requested. Note the plural listing, once again, of parents, students, teachers; this is not accidental. A broad range of interests and individuals should be represented. The council should include parents, students and teachers from all levels: elementary, middle and secondary schools.

Pupil services personnel includes guidance and counseling professionals, school nurse, psychologists and school social workers.

Appropriate state agencies can be any state agency that deals with children, families, ATOD, health or social services. Many state agencies maintain regional offices with personnel who work locally.

Private schools should include representatives from nonpublic schools in the area, including preschools and nurseries.

Medical professionals generally refers to health services staff, including, but not limited to medical doctor, registered nurse, dentist, chiropractor or other licensed/certified professional.

Law enforcement can include sheriff, police, probation department, judge or hearing officer, district attorney or federal agent.

Community-based organizations refers to parent/teacher organizations, the American Cancer Society, American Heart Association, YMCA, YWCA, Girl Scouts, Boy Scouts, Lions and Rotary clubs, and the Elks and Masons.

Groups with interest/expertise in drug and violence prevention is meant to encompass a host of other organizations, such as the youth bureau and drug treatment centers.

SOLICITING MEMBERSHIP

The letter announcing formation of an advisory council should briefly state the purpose and responsibilities of the committee and invite participation. Include criteria for selection of members, with a time line. The importance of the committee and its charge will be duly noted if the letter is sent under the Board President or Superintendent's signature.

Create a "prospects" mailing list that includes individuals, agencies and organizations whose representation is required by the Safe and Drug-Free Schools Act (SDFSCA). Include a sentence or two about membership terms in the invitation letter. It is advisable to appoint individuals for staggered one-, two- or three-year terms. This provides flexibility to recruit other people and also allows current members to serve additional terms, thus assuring continuity. Once the panel has been established, additional procedures can be developed.

Create an application form to attach to the letter and include a due date on the form. The form might ask for the following:

- basic data (e.g., name, address, telephone number)
- affiliation with the school district (if any)
- a paragraph describing how the person can contribute to the advisory council
- educational background
- current employer name, address and telephone number
- special expertise or interests
- commitment and ability to attend meetings (quarterly or more frequently, if necessary. Evening meetings are suggested although afternoons or rotating time may work well.)

Allow a week beyond the due date for receipt of applications, then begin to sort the forms. An ad hoc committee should consider the categories of membership required by the SDFSA as a guide to separating applications. An individual may represent more than one field of expertise if it is necessary to limit the number of people who are selected. A "parent" can also be a "local law enforcement official." Be aware, however, that while efficient to use an individual in this manner, it may narrow the range of opinion and possibly compromise the overall goals of broad community involvement.

Send a letter congratulating those selected to serve on the DAC and include the date, time and location of the first meeting. Others should receive a letter thanking them for their interest, acknowledging the large number of applicants and inviting their reapplication in the future, if appropriate.

SELECTING MEMBERS

Consider the criteria for selecting and appointing members of the DAC. Reflect on the following suggested criteria, adapted from The Texas Association for Health, Physical Education, Recreation and Dance's publication *Health Education Advisory Councils: A Checklist for Success:*

☑ **Demonstrated interest in youth**

Has the individual previously participated in an activity to help children or adolescents?

☑ **Awareness of community culture and needs**

Does the individual bring an awareness of important issues, such as culture, politics, geography and economy?

☑ **Professional abilities**

Does the prospective member offer specific expertise?

☑ **Willingness to devote time**

A sincere desire to attend meetings and be an active contributor should be considered one of the key qualifications for membership.

☑ **Representative of population**

Seek balance, diversity and richness in the DAC by seeking out people who represent as many segments of the population as possible.

CHECKLIST

Date Completed

- ☐ Examine logistics: districtwide Health Advisory Council with subcommittees versus separate Drug Advisory Council   _____
- ☐ Initial leadership by board/administration   _____
- ☐ Develop criteria for selection of council members   _____
- ☐ Call for members/application   _____
- ☐ Selection of members   _____
- ☐ Appointment of members who represent categories required by ESEA Title IV Safe and Drug-Free Schools and Communities   _____

Chapter 8

ADVISORY COUNCIL
ROLES AND RESPONSIBILITIES

ADVISORY CAPACITY

As described by federal law, the SDFSCA Drug Advisory Council serves in an advisory capacity. In its advisory role, the council can gather information and resources, study specific topics or issues, produce reports, take on projects, and work with schools and agencies to improve health and safety. The DAC makes recommendations, and the power of its membership can help make its views heard by the administration and the community.

Do not confuse the DAC with a policymaking group, such as the school board or the policy development committee described in Chapter 2. Policy is not the DAC's *mandated* role, although the group certainly can serve schools as policy consultants.

In fact, DACs are remarkably versatile beyond their SDFSCA-mandated responsibilities. DAC members may take on additional duties, such as representing the district on a community task force, attending public hearings, speaking to parent organizations, working on school improvement plans, serving as liaison to the student assistance program or core team, or making presentations to the school board.

The DAC is authorized by the Safe and Drug-Free Schools Act to perform at least six basic functions. These duties are not financial in nature, but rather focus on programs, networking and communication.

RESPONSIBILITIES OUTLINED UNDER ESEA TITLE IV: SAFE AND DRUG-FREE SCHOOLS ACT

Section 4115 (see Appendix A) clearly describes the functions for the district advisory council. The following are the duties as defined by law:

1. Assist With the Development of the District's SDFSCA Grant Application

Districts that receive the SDFSCA grant application from the state department of education generally have 90 days to return it. This does not mean that all work must be done in 90 days. The advisory council can prepare much of the information ahead of time and submit it to the grantwriter. For instance, the grant requires that the district assess current levels of ATOD use and violence. The DAC can help gather and analyze the data in preparation for the application. The SDFSCA grant also requires evaluation of prevention programs and activities. The advisory council may assume some of this responsibility or work with an outside evaluator and use the report for program recommendations.

2. Publicize and Promote the District's ATOD and Violence Prevention Activities

This may be one of the DAC's most important activities, because it can help boost recognition and use of the district's efforts. To clarify this point, imagine that the middle school is beginning a peer leadership program, but very few students step forward for training. DAC members can promote the project and ask their friends to tell their children about it. The council's networking would help launch and nurture the program.

3. Help the District to Coordinate DAC Efforts With Similar Programs and Projects

Avoid duplication of services through coordination. Council members with experience and connections within the school and community can work with the district to create a collaborative work plan with minimal overlap. As an example, the district may not be aware of community-sponsored tutoring for elementary school students, but one of the DAC members may be a program volunteer who can share her experiences. Because academic failure is one of the research-based risk factors for early ATOD use, connecting with this program could be an important addition to the district's prevention program.

4. Offer Advice and Input Regarding Agencies That Work With Schools in the Areas of ATOD and Violence Prevention

DAC members often have experience working with community groups and can provide valuable links. For instance, the school may benefit from a new program offered by the local American Lung Association. Or a nationally-known speaker may move into town, and a member of the advisory council can bring this to the attention of the district. The council can be the "eyes and ears" of the school district, looking for services and programs that will benefit students, staff and families.

5. Review Evaluation of Programs and Projects

Does the service learning program in the 10th grade promote positive attributes in the participants? Has the conflict mediation program in the elementary school reached its goals of reducing physical fights, bullying and oral threats? The council can review program evaluations, discuss alternatives and make recommendations to the district that answer these questions.

6. Recommend Improvements or Modifications to the District's Prevention Programs

As an advisory group, the council has no specific powers. But it can examine the performance of the district's programs and make recommendations. For instance, as the council reviews K-6 prevention efforts, it is determined that the elementary school staff's most recent training in a specific curriculum occurred eight years ago. Twelve new teachers have been hired since, and the curriculum was upgraded last year. Council members may suggest that the district investigate to see if more training is needed. Or it may be that the districtwide survey of drugs and violence revealed a large jump between grades 6 and 8 in the numbers of students using marijuana. National surveys, such as *Monitoring the Future* and *PRIDE,* have found this to be the case. The DAC may examine the latest district survey and recommend that the district be proactive by adding more prevention programs and activities for grades 5, 6, 7 and 8 into the curriculum.

SCOPE/ORIENTATION

A group functions best with a common purpose and a common base of knowledge and experience. Before work commences, have the DAC review the school mission/vision, and the Goals 2000 national Goal 7:

Goal 7

> *Every school in the United States will be free of drugs, violence, and the unauthorized presence of firearms and alcohol, and will offer a disciplined environment conducive to learning.*

Read and distribute the DAC's governing ordinance, Safe and Drug-Free Schools Act, Title IV, Section 4115 (a) (2) as part of the initial meeting. (See Appendix A.) The group should also consider developing a council mission statement. Upon completion of this mission statement, make copies for each member, and post it at work sessions.

Plan for scheduled meetings of the full advisory council, with subcommittee meetings as needed, and develop a plan of work for the year. It is important that the DAC be careful not to take on too much responsibility or it will risk "burning out" its members. Projects can be prioritized and undertaken as needed.

At the first meeting of the year, select dates for the year's remaining meetings and send them to members with meeting minutes.

WORKING TOGETHER

As a practical matter, the chairperson who facilitates DAC meetings must be proficient at working with diverse populations. Open a dialogue to establish ground rules for how your group will work. Some DACs adopt bylaws or rules of order to guide their functions. Others operate informally, tabling program discussion when conflict, not content, dominates the floor. All councils will, at one time or another, need to examine their group process.

MINUTES/RECORDS

All organizations need clear, up-to-date records. The DAC chairperson should dedicate a file and notebook for advisory council business and keep it current. Dated copies of all materials, handouts, minutes and reports belong there and may be organized by subject or kept in chronological order.

Because the chairperson facilitates the meeting, another member should record and transcribe notes and prepare minutes. Distribute minutes as soon as possible after each meeting and file additional copies for later use.

ADDITIONAL DUTIES OR PROJECTS

One of the most important duties of the advisory council is improving drug and violence prevention programs and projects. The council members represent a cross section of individuals, professions and interests. Their contributions can be invaluable.

For instance, the district may wish to become a "Drug-Free School Zone." Federal law provides for double penalties in instances of drug-related felonies committed on school property or within 1,000 feet of school boundary lines. This multifaceted project requires the cooperation of the school, law enforcement and local government, cooperation the DAC can facilitate. (See Appendix E for resources and information.)

The DAC may coordinate this project, shepherding it from inception to implementation, through levels of bureaucracy and approvals. Even after "Drug-Free School Zone" signs are in place, the process is not yet complete. An awareness campaign must be initiated to promote the zones, and strategic alliances should be established to ensure that the zones are patrolled and enforced. This project can be handled smoothly and efficiently by the advisory council.

COUNCIL MEMBERS AS PROGRAM ADVOCATES

DAC members' involvement and efforts can spur them to become advocates for the school's prevention goals and programs. Consider this example: The local newspaper may be researching a story on youth violence. A reporter calls the school to learn what is being done about this issue. The superintendent may ask a member of the DAC to describe to the reporter the school-based programs and coordination with community violence prevention efforts, including the Advisory Council's ongoing work. Because of their involvement, these people talk to colleagues, friends and neighbors about their work on the DAC. This positive "word-of-mouth" is a valuable asset!

PUBLIC RELATIONS

Public relations (PR) has become an important aspect of school-community relations. With personnel, resources and budgets stretched to the limit, it is critical to let the public know how the district is acting on behalf of students, staff and families. By using the advisory council process, a district demonstrates the ability to respond to community needs and interests.

Publicizing the DAC's work is not just positive PR, it is part of an ongoing effort to inform, promote and collaborate with parents and the community.

REPORTING PROCEDURES

The DAC can select from several options for reporting its work: oral, written, outline or a combination. Written reports need not be extensive or formal. They should be produced annually, at a minimum.

Members may elect to send an outline of the year's work or draft a report of specific projects and send copies to district decisionmakers. A representative can make an oral presentation to administrators or the school board, answer questions and report back to the full DAC. For wider distribution, outlines or reports can be appended to the district Web site or become part of the school board's minutes.

CONTINUITY

Members' terms of service may vary, but, as recommended in Chapter 7, consider staggered, renewable one-, two- and three-year appointments. This will help to keep some core members in place and also assure the district of a greater variety of views and expertise.

Because of the changing nature of the DAC, accurate and complete records must be kept. Historical documents avoid duplication of effort and "reinventing the wheel" syndrome that is so regularly encountered.

The first meeting of each year's new DAC should feature a brief, 10-minute presentation and orientation to the previous Council's projects and accomplishments. To become familiar with Council process and procedures, new members may welcome the opportunity to look at past years' reports and minutes, which should be made readily available to them.

As advisory council members change, consider the need for an orientation program and a drug prevention update. When the district or community conducts a survey of ATOD and violence, make certain that the council gets the results. Invite DAC members to participate in the district's staff development training, particularly as it pertains to ATOD issues. Council members need to feel that they are a vital part of the district's efforts to reduce ATOD risks.

	CHECKLIST	Date Completed
❏	Review and clarify responsibilities and duties	_____
❏	Provide a group orientation	
❏	Define the Council's advisory capacity	_____
❏	Keep records and organize materials	_____
❏	Use the DAC for positive public relations	_____
❏	Make recommendations in writing	_____
❏	Plan for continuity	_____

SAMPLE AGENDAS FOR DRUG ADVISORY COUNCIL
4 meetings per school year (average)

First Meeting
Suggested time period for first meeting: 1¹/2 hours
Refreshments should be provided.

Welcome, introductions .... 10 minutes
Overview of Goal 7 and Title IV: Safe and
     Drug-Free Schools Act .... 5 minutes
Description, discussion of statutory duties,
     responsibilities .... 15 minutes
Organizational issues .... 15 minutes
     Leadership: appointed/elected/rotating chairperson(s)
     Record keeping: note taking, writing minutes, sending
          minutes/reminders
     Methods for developing agendas and work plans for future
          meetings
     Communication between DAC members

Background information .... 20 minutes
> Outline of district's health education program
> Outline of district's current drug/violence prevention
> programs and activities
> Presentation of latest survey/assessment data on
> drug/violence (when available)
> Identification of key professionals in school-based
> substance abuse/violence prevention: health educators,
> student assistance team, school social worker, safety
> officer, school psychologist, counselors, health services
> personnel, etc.

Review of district's current SDFSCA grant .... 10 minutes
Schedule next meeting; begin to build agenda .... 10 minutes
Closure .... 5 minutes

- *Minutes should be sent out no later than 1 week after each DAC meeting.*
- *Ask members to call with agenda items for the next meeting at least 3 days ahead of the meeting date.*
- *Suggestions for 2nd meeting: invite several "key informants" to address the advisory council (see page 12). A panel of 3–4 individuals can be assembled; each can be asked to prepare a 3–4 minute statement and then answer questions. See page 12–13 for sample topics.*

Second Meeting
Suggested time period for second meeting: 2 hours
Refreshments should be provided.

Welcome, introductions, agenda distribution .... 10 minutes
Review of minutes .... 5 minutes
Key informants panel (including Q&A) .... 45 minutes
Discussion period .... 10 minutes
Agenda items requested by DAC members .... varies
Organizational issues .... 20 minutes
> Developing a mission statement
> Forming subcommittees for special tasks, if desired
> Raising concerns
> Other

Setting date for next meeting, beginning to build
     agenda . . . . 10 minutes
Closure . . . . 5 minutes

- *Minutes should be sent out no later than 1 week after each DAC meeting.*
- *Ask members to call with agenda items for the next meeting at least 3 days ahead of the meeting date.*
- *Suggestion for 3rd meeting: Review pages 58–60 for duties defined for the Drug Advisory Council under the Safe and Drug-Free Schools Act. Discuss specific projects for the DAC. For instance, members can research and compile a list of state and national commemorations related to drugs and violence. Some of these include Alcoholism Awareness Month (April) and Red Ribbon Week (last week in October). Perhaps the Council is interested in reviewing prevention programs grade by grade to gain a better understanding of the district's overall efforts. Or the group may decide that they are particularly concerned about the increase in violence and drug abuse at times of transition from middle school to high school and focus time and energy on this issue.*

Third Meeting
Suggested time period for second meeting: 2 hours
Refreshments should be provided.

Welcome, introductions, agenda distribution . . . . 5 minutes
Review of minutes . . . . 5 minutes
Finalization of mission statement . . . . 15 minutes
Introduction of ideas, discussion of future plans
     and projects . . . . 40 minutes
Organizing for project(s) . . . . 15 minutes
Agenda items requested by DAC members . . . . varies
Thinking ahead for the next year's SDFSCA grant . . . 10 minutes
Organizational issues . . . . 15 minutes
     Preparing for final meeting of school year
     Making recommendations for next year's DAC
     Nominating/rotating members

Setting date for next meeting, beginning to build
    agenda .... 10 minutes
Closure .... 5 minutes

- *Minutes should be sent out no later than 1 week after each DAC meeting.*
- *Ask members to call with agenda items for the next meeting at least 3 days ahead of the meeting date.*
- *Suggestions for 4th meeting: This would be an ideal time to celebrate the completion of the year's work, and lay the foundation for the coming year. The DAC should evaluate itself, looking at such issues as organization, operations, effectiveness, efficiency, personnel, duties and future potential for success.*

Fourth Meeting
Suggested time period for second meeting: 1¹/2 hours
Refreshments should be provided.

Welcome, introductions, agenda distribution .... 5 minutes
Review of minutes .... 5 minutes
A look back: .... 10 minutes
    What have we accomplished?
    What have we learned?
A look ahead: .... 20 minutes
    How can we improve the workings of the DAC?
    What should we concentrate on next year?
    What challenges are still facing us?
    What recommendations (if any) shall we make to the
       district?
Membership: going, coming, soliciting new
    members .... 10 minutes
Review of the district's Safe and Drug-Free Schools
    grant application .... 15 minutes
Agenda items requested by DAC members .... varies
Setting date for next meeting, beginning to build
    agenda .... 10 minutes
Closure .... 5 minutes

- *Minutes should be sent out no later than 1 week after each DAC meeting.*
- *Ask members to call with agenda items for the next meeting at least 3 days ahead of the meeting date.*

Appendix A

ESEA TITLE IV SECTION 4115 (A)(1)(2): SAFE AND DRUG-FREE SCHOOLS AND COMMUNITIES ACT

SEC. 4115. LOCAL APPLICATIONS

(a) Application Required.—

(1) In general.—In order to be eligible to receive a distribution under section 4113(d) for any fiscal year, a local educational agency shall submit, at such time as the State educational agency requires, an application to the State educational agency for approval. Such an application shall be amended, as necessary, to reflect changes in the local educational agency's program.

(2) Development.—

(A) A local educational agency shall develop its application under subsection (a)(1) in consultation with a local or sub-state regional advisory council that includes, to the extent possible, representatives of local government, business, parents, students, teachers, pupil services personnel, appropriate State agencies, private schools, the medical profession, law enforcement, community-based organizations, and other groups with interest and expertise in drug and violence prevention.

(B) In addition to assisting the local educational agency to develop an application under this section, the advisory council established or designated under subparagraph (A) shall, on an ongoing basis—

(i) disseminate information about drug and violence prevention programs, projects, and activities conducted
within the boundaries of the local educational agency;

(ii) advise the local educational agency regarding—

(I) how best to coordinate such agency's activities
under this subpart with other related programs,
projects, and activities; and

(II) the agencies that administer such programs, projects, and activities; and

(iii) review program evaluations and other relevant material and make recommendations to the local educational agency on how to improve such agency's drug
and violence prevention programs.

Appendix B

GOALS 2000
PART C—ENVIRONMENTAL
TOBACCO SMOKE
(PRO-CHILDREN ACT OF 1994)

SEC. 1043 NONSMOKING POLICY
FOR CHILDREN'S SERVICES

(a) *PROHIBITION.*—After the date of the enactment of this Act, no person shall permit smoking within any indoor facility owned or leased or contracted for and used by such person for provision of routine or regular kindergarten, elementary, or secondary education or library services to children.

(b) *ADDITIONAL PROHIBITION.*—After the date of the enactment of this Act, no person shall permit smoking within any indoor facility (or portion thereof) owned or leased or contracted for by such person for the provision of regular or routine health care or day care or early childhood development (Head Start) services to children or for the use of the employees of such person who provides such services, except that this subsection shall not apply to—

    (1) any portion of such facility that is used for inpatient hospital treatment of individuals dependent on, or addicted to, drugs or alcohol; and

    (2) any private residence

(c) *FEDERAL AGENCIES.*—

    (1) KINDERGARTEN, ELEMENTARY, OR SECONDARY EDUCATION OR LIBRARY SERVICES.—After the date of the enactment of this Act, no Federal agency shall permit smoking within any indoor facility operated by such

agency, directly or by contract, to provide routine or regular kindergarten, elementary or secondary education or library services to children.

(2) HEALTH OR DAY CARE OR EARLY CHILDHOOD DEVELOPMENT SERVICES.—After the date of the enactment of this Act, no Federal agency shall permit smoking within any indoor facility (or portion thereof) operated by such agency, directly or by contract, to provide routine or regular health or day care or early childhood development (Head Start) services to children, except that this paragraph shall not apply to—

   (A) any portion of such facility that is used for inpatient hospital treatment of individuals dependent on, or addicted to, drugs or alcohol; and

   (B) any private residence.

(3) *APPLICATION OF PROVISIONS.*—The provisions of paragraph (2) shall also apply to the provision of such routine or regular kindergarten, elementary or secondary education or library services in the facilities described in paragraph (2) not subject to paragraph (1).

Appendix C

SAFE AND DRUG-FREE SCHOOLS PRINCIPLES OF EFFECTIVENESS

(Final version, as published in the Federal Register,
vol. 63 no. 104, June 1, 1998)

Having safe and drug-free schools is one of our Nation's highest priorities. To ensure that recipients of Title IV funds use those funds in ways that preserve State and local flexibility but are most likely to reduce drug use and violence among youth, a recipient shall coordinate its SDFSCA funded programs with other available prevention efforts to maximize the impact of all the drug and violence prevention programs and resources available to its State, school district, or community, and shall —

- *Base its programs on a thorough assessment of objective data about the drug and violence problems in the schools and communities served.* Each SDFSCA grant recipient shall conduct a thorough assessment of the nature and extent of youth drug use and violence problems. Grantees are encouraged to build on existing data collection efforts and examine available objective data from a variety of sources, including law enforcement and public health officials. Grantees are encouraged to assess the needs of all segments of the youth population. While information about the availability of relevant services in the community and schools is an important part of any needs assessment, and while grantees may wish to include data on adult drug use and violence problems, grantees shall, at a minimum, include in the needs assessment data on youth drug use and violence;

- *With the assistance of a local or regional advisory council where required by the SDFSCA, establish a set of measurable goals and objectives and design its programs*

73

to meet those goals and objectives. Sections 4112 and 4115 of the SDFSCA require that grantees develop measurable goals and objectives for their programs. Grantees shall develop goals and objectives that focus on behavioral or attitudinal program outcomes, as well as on program implementation (sometimes called "process data"). While measures of implementation (such as the hours of instruction provided or number of teachers trained) are important, they are not sufficient to measure program outcomes. Grantees shall develop goals and objectives that permit them to determine the extent to which programs are effective in reducing or preventing drug use, violence, or disruptive behavior among youth;

- *Design and implement its programs for youth based on research or evaluation that provides evidence that the programs used prevent or reduce drug use, violence, or disruptive behavior among youth.* In designing and improving its youth programs, a grant recipient shall taking into consideration its needs assessment and measurable goals and objectives, select and implement programs for youth that have demonstrated effectiveness or promise of effectiveness, in preventing or reducing drug use, violence, or disruptive behavior, or other behaviors or attitudes demonstrated to be precursors to or predictors of drug use or violence. While the Secretary recognizes the importance of flexibility in addressing State and local needs, the Secretary believes that the implementation of research-based programs will significantly enhance the effectiveness of programs supported with SDFSCA funds. In selecting effective programs most responsive to their needs, grantees are encouraged to review the breadth of available research and evaluation literature, and to replicate these programs in a manner consistent with their original design, and

- *Evaluate its programs periodically to assess its progress toward achieving its goals and objectives, and use its evaluation results to refine, improve, and strengthen its program, and to refine its goals and objectives as appro-*

priate. Grant recipients shall assess their programs and use the information about program outcomes and fidelity of replication to re-evaluate existing program efforts. The Secretary recognizes that prevention programs may have a long implementation phase, may have long-term goals, and may include some objectives that are broadly focused. However, grantees shall not continue to use SDF-SCA funds to implement programs that cannot demonstrate positive outcomes in terms of reducing or preventing drug use, violence, or disruptive behavior among youth, or other behaviors or attitudes demonstrated to be precursors to or predictors of drug use or violence. Grantees shall use their assessment results to determine whether programs need to be strengthened or improved, and whether program goals and objectives are reasonable or have already been met and should be revised. Consistent with Sections 4112 and 4115 of the SDFSCA, grant recipients shall report to the public on progress toward attaining measurable goals and objectives for drug and violence prevention.

Appendix D

CASE HISTORIES FOR DISTRICT DRUG POLICY

The cases located in this section are designed to stimulate effective drug policy development.

Whether developing new policies or revising current policies, before setting to work ask policy committee members to role-play each case study. Role playing will provoke creative reasoning and may highlight specific points for discussion.

Use the cases several times to help members focus and clarify their thoughts, asking different people to assume the roles. Once policies and procedures have been drafted, walk through each case history to test them.

Staff members can role play the cases as a check on their level of understanding and ability to implement new policies/procedures. Use case studies for annual review and skills update.

Basic players have been listed for each case, but, if needed, additional people may be added to the cast. Suggestions for additional players: school nurse, dean of students, police officer and student assistance counselor.

CASE STUDY 1

Players:
Kim, 10th grade student
Mrs. Smith, school secretary
Mr. Tate, high school principal
Ross & Trudy Gulino, Kim's parents

Kim goes to the principal's office to ask Mrs. Smith for a late pass. Mrs. Smith notices the strong odor of alcohol on Kim's breath.

A) What, if anything, should Mrs. Smith say to Kim?

B) What should Mrs. Smith do immediately?

C) Who should Mrs. Smith tell about the incident?

D) Who should interview Kim and what should that person say, specifically?

E) Will Kim's parents be notified? By whom? What should be said?

F) What are Kim's consequences as a result of this incident?

G) Will any ATOD assessment or referral be recommended?

H) Should Mrs. Smith make a written report? Who gets the report?

I) Point out the specific discipline/policy excerpts that apply to this situation.

CASE STUDY 2

Players:
Nick, 9th grade student
Coach Peters
Louise Hunt, Nick's mother

Coach Peters and the basketball team are returning from a Saturday semifinal game. The bus stops at a rest stop along the highway. When Coach Peters comes out of the bathroom he sees Nick quickly flick a smoking cigarette away.

A) What, if anything, should Coach Peters say to Nick?

B) What should Coach Peters do?

C) Who should Coach Peters tell about the incident?

D) Who should interview Nick and what should that person say?

E) Should Nick's mother be notified? By whom? What should be said?

F) What are Nick's consequences as a result of this incident?

G) Will any ATOD assessment or referral be recommended?

H) Point out the specific discipline/policy citations that apply to this situation.

CASE STUDY 3

Players:
Mrs. Wentworth, middle school guidance counselor
Tisha, Cecilia, 8th grade students
Morris Moore, Tisha's father
Betty Wong, Cecilia's mother

Mrs. Wentworth passes the girls' bathroom and notices a strong odor that smells like marijuana to her. She enters and sees smoke coming out of one of the stalls. She knocks on the door and tells the students to come out immediately. She hears a flush and two girls unlock the stall door. They smell like smoke, but neither has anything in her hand, although each has a purse on her shoulder.

A) What should Mrs. Wentworth say and do immediately?

B) To whom should this incident be reported? How is the report made?

C) Who, if anyone, should interview the girls?

D) Should the girls be searched for marijuana or paraphernalia such as rolling paper? If yes, by whom and how?

E) Who should call the parents and what should be said?

F) What are the consequences to each girl as a result of this incident?

G) Will any ATOD assessment or referral be recommended?

H) Point out the specific discipline/policy excerpts that apply to this situation.

CASE STUDY 4

Players:
Mr. Baker, high school assistant principal
Terry, 10th grade student
Stacy, 11th grade student
Chantal Hendricks, Terry's mother
Harriet Gardner, Stacy's mother

In the school cafeteria during lunch period, Mr. Baker, the assistant principal, sees Terry give Stacy two pills.

    A) What, if anything, should Mr. Baker say and do immediately?

    B) Who should this incident be reported to? How is the report made?

    C) Who, if anyone, should interview the students?

    D) Should the students be searched for pills and/or other substances? If yes, by whom and how?

    E) Who should call the parents and what should be said?

    F) What are the consequences to Terry as a result of this incident? What are the consequences to Stacy as a result of this incident?

    G) Will any ATOD assessment or referral be recommended?

    H) Point out the specific discipline/policy excerpts that apply to this situation.

CASE STUDY 5

Players:
Mr. Sherman, high school bus driver
Buddy, Slade, 10th grade students
Juan & Cindy Pappas, Buddy's parents
Lila Turner, Slade's mother

As Mr. Sherman prepares to pull out of the school driveway, he glances in the rear view mirror. He notices Buddy giving Slade several dollar bills, sees Slade hand Buddy a small, shiny foil packet. Mr. Sherman suspects that this is a drug sale.

    A) What should Mr. Sherman say to Buddy or Slade? What should Mr. Sherman do immediately?

    B) Who should Mr. Sherman tell about the incident?

    C) Who should interview the boys and what should be discussed?

D) Will the police be notified? If yes, when? Who will do this?

E) Are the parents notified? By whom? What should be said?

F) What are the consequences to Buddy as a result of this incident? What are the consequences to Slade as a result of this incident?

G) Will any ATOD assessment or referral be recommended?

H) Point out the specific sections of discipline/policy excerpts that apply to this situation.

CASE STUDY 6

Players:
Allison, high school senior
Mrs. Nichols, hall monitor
Melaine Walker, Allison's mother

As Mrs. Nichols checks the corridors after the first period late bell, she comes around the corner and sees Allison standing by her locker. Allison has a bottle in a bag and is drinking from it. She looks down the hallway, then puts the bag into her locker. Mrs. Nichols walks over to Allison as she locks her locker and notes the smell of beer.

A) What should Mrs. Nichols say and do immediately?

B) Who should Mrs. Nichols tell about this incident?

C) Who should interview Allison? Who should be present at the interview?

D) Should Allison's locker be searched? If yes, by whom and under what circumstances?

E) Who should call Allison's mother and what should be said?

F) What are the consequences to Allison as a result of this incident?

G) Will any ATOD assessment or referral be recommended?

H) Point out the specific discipline/policy citations that apply to this situation.

CASE STUDY 7

Players:
Jo-Jo, Teddy, Hank 12th grade students
Ms. Crawford, senior class advisor
Mr. Webster, parent chaperone
Mary Williams, Jo-Jo's mother
Ted & Frances Stevens, Teddy's parents
Ken Hart, Hank's father

Jo-Jo, Teddy and Hank are roommates on the senior class trip. At midnight Ms. Crawford makes her last "bed check." When she knocks on their door she gets no response so assumes they have fallen asleep. The next morning none of the boys is at breakfast, so Ms. Crawford calls their room. After six rings, Jo-Jo answers but his speech is slow and slurred. Mr. Webster and Ms. Crawford go immediately to the boys' room. Jo-Jo opens the door looking dazed and unsteady. Teddy and Hank are stretched out on one bed, fully clothed. Jo-Jo can't remember where he is and can't answer simple questions.

A) What, if anything, should Ms. Crawford say and do immediately?

B) Is medical intervention indicated? If so, how will this be handled, and by whom?

C) Who should this incident be reported to? How is the report made?

D) Who, if anyone, should interview the students?

E) Should the students be searched for pills and/or other substances? If yes, by whom and how?

F) Who should call the parents and what should be said?

G) What are the consequences to each student as a result of this incident? Will any ATOD assessment or referral be recommended?

H) Point out specific portions of discipline/policy excerpts that apply to this situation.

CASE STUDY 8

Players:
Mr. Thurman, art teacher
Lashanda, Violet, 6th grade students

While the sixth grade class works on their art projects, Lashanda and Violet spill rubber cement on their table and rub their hands in it. They hold their hands over their faces, breathing deep and giggling. Mr. Thurman smells the strong odor of cement and sees the girls laughing uncontrollably. They tell him they are "huffing."

A) What, if anything, should Mr. Thurman say and do immediately?

B) To whom should this incident be reported? How should the report be made?

C) Should anyone interview the students? Who?

D) Is medical assistance indicated?

E) Who should call the parents and what should be said?

F) What are the consequences to both girls as a result of this incident?

G) Will any ATOD assessment or referral be recommended?

H) Cite the specific discipline/policy segments that apply to this situation.

CASE STUDY 9

Players:
Nelson, a 9th grade student
Mr. Tyler, study hall supervisor
Dr. Santiago, high school principal
Cassandra and Anthony Brown, Nelson's parents

Nelson has been in some minor trouble at school previously, disciplined for a fistfight and using foul language when speaking to a teacher. Yesterday, Nelson bragged to some friends about how many drugs he could get. In period 5 study hall, he showed students a collection of pills in a sandwich bag. Mr. Tyler saw the bag, confiscated it and took it to Dr. Santiago. The next morning, Nelson's parents are meeting with Dr. Santiago to discuss the incident. Nelson's parents are very angry and insist that Nelson was "framed" by Mr. Tyler or someone else at the school.

A) Cite the specific discipline/policy segments that apply to this situation.

B) Is there a written report of this incident? Where is it and where will it be stored? Is access restricted?

C) What are the consequences to Nelson as a result of this incident?

D) Who, if anyone, should be at this meeting besides Dr. Santiago and the Browns?

E) What should Dr. Santiago say to Mr. and Mrs. Brown?

F) Where is the bag with pills? What will be done with it?

G) Will law enforcement authorities be contacted? When and by whom?

CASE STUDY 10

Players:
George, Laura, Peter, Renee, high school seniors
Mr. Kay, high school principal
Mr. Lawlor, assistant superintendent
+ others as needed

Mr. Kay and Mr. Lawlor are curbside in front of the ballroom, welcoming students to the senior prom. As announced weeks before, their job is to stand by the door as each vehicle pulls up and scan the inside for alcoholic beverages. When George, Laura, Peter and Renee get out of their vehicle, something shiny catches Mr. Kay's eye. He sees Peter toss a silver beer can under the velvet car seat, and he can see several other shiny cans there as well.

A) What should Mr. Kay or Mr. Lawlor say or do immediately?

B) May the limousine be searched? If yes, by whom?

C) Should students be questioned? What should be asked? Will there be a written record? Will there be witnesses?

D) To whom should this incident be reported?

E) Who should call the parents and what should be said?

F) What are the consequences for Peter as a result of this incident? Are there any consequences to the other students?

G) Will any ATOD assessment or referral be recommended?

H) Point out the sections of the discipline code or policy that apply to this situation.

Appendix E

RESOURCES

The material in this appendix is not intended to be a complete, exhaustive or all-inclusive list of available resources, agencies or organizations. Legal advice should only be obtained from your school attorney.

1. *Fit, Healthy, and Ready to Learn: A School Health Policy Guide,* J. Bogden, National Association of State Boards of Education, 2000. (800-220-5183; www.nasbe.org).

2. *Student Violence,* ed. by T. Hoffman, Looseleaf Law Publications, Inc., 1997. (41-23 150th St., Fresh Meadows, NY 11355, 718-359-5559, www.Looseleaf Law.com)

3. *The Disciplinarian's Handbook,* by L. Fennessy, Looseleaf Law Publications, Inc., 1997. (See above)

4. *Creating a Safe and Drug-Free School: An Action Guide,* U.S. Department of Education, U.S. Department of Justice, 1996. (available through NCADI and the U.S. Department of Education)

5. *Handbook of Legal Issues for School-Based Programs,* by Legal Action Center, 1996. (153 Waverly Place, NY, NY 10014, 212-243-1313)

6. *Health Education Advisory Councils: A Checklist for Success,* ed. By B.E. Pruitt, D.C. Wiley, J.R. Jonas, Texas Association for Health, Physical Education, Recreation & Dance, 1996. (TAHPERD, 6300 La Calma Drive Suite 100, Austin TX 78752, 512-459-1299, quentin@tahperd.org)

7. *Making Your Workplace Drug Free,* Substance Abuse and Mental Health Services Administration/Center for Substance Abuse Prevention, undated. (available through CSAP Workplace Helpline, 1-800-WORKPLACE.)

8. *Drug-Free Schools and Children: A Primer for School Policymakers,* American Council for Drug Education, undated. (164 W. 74th St. NY, NY 10023, 800-488-DRUG, www.acde.org)

9. *The Michigan Guide to School Policies and Programs on Alcohol and Other Drugs,* Michigan Dept. of Education & Michigan Office of Substance Abuse Services, 1991

10. *No Kidding Around! America's Young Activist Are Changing Our World,* Information USA, 1992. (Activism 2000, PO Box E, Kensington, MD, 20895, 301-929-8808)

11. *A Practical Guide for Administrators and Educators for Combating Drug and Alcohol Abuse,* 2nd edition. by John F. Lewis, et al., National Organization on Legal Problems of Education, 1992.

12. *A Framework for Prevention: A Guide for Developing a Comprehensive School Policy concerning Alcohol and Other Substances,* New York State Education Department, 1990.

13. *School Discipline Policies and Procedures: A Practical Guide (Revised),* by Frels, Kelly et al, National School Boards Association, 1990.

FEDERAL AGENCIES

Centers for Disease Control and Prevention	404-639-3311	www.cdc.gov
Center for Substance Abuse Prevention Drug-Free Workplace Helpline	800-843-4971 800-967-5752	www.samhsa.gov/csap helpline@samhsa.gov
Drug Information and Strategy Clearinghouse	800-578-3472	www.hud.gov
Drug Information and Strategy Clearinghouse	800-578-3472	www.hud.gov
Juvenile Justice Clearinghouse	800-638-8736	www.ncjrs.org/ojjhome.htm
National Clearinghouse for Alcohol and Drug Information (NCADI)	800-729-6686	www.health.org
National Criminal Justice Information Center	800-851-3420	www.ncjrs.org
National Institute on Drug Abuse	800-729-6686	www.nida.nih.gov
National Mental Health Services Knowledge Exchange Network	800-789-2647	www.mentalhealth.org
Office of Juvenile Justice and Delinquency Prevention	202-307-5911	www.ncjrs.org/ojjhome.htm
Office of National Drug Control Policy	800-666-3332	www.whitehousedrugpolicy.gov
U.S. Department of Education Safe & Drug Free Schools	202-260-3954	www.ed.gov/offices/OESE/SDFS
U.S. Department of Labor Workplace Substance Abuse Programs	202-219-8211	www.dol.gov/dol/asp/public/programs/drugs/main.htm

NATIONAL ORGANIZATIONS

American Council for Drug Education	800-488-DRUG	www.acde.org
Center on Addiction and Substance Abuse at Columbia University	212-841-5200	www.casacolumbia.org
Center for Science in the Public Interest	202-332-9110	www.cspi.net
Center for Substance Abuse Research	301-403-8329	www.bsos.umd.edu/cesar/cesar.html
Community Anti-Drug Coalitions of America (CADCA)	800-54-CADCA	www.cadca.org/cadcahom.htm
Join Together	617-437-1500	www.jointogether.org
Mothers Against Drunk Driving	800-438-6233	www.madd.org
National Alliance for Model State Drug Laws	703-836-6100	www.natlalliance.org/
National Council on Alcoholism and Drug Dependence	212-206-6770	www.ncadd.org
National Families in Action	770-934-6364	www.emory.edu/NFIA
National Inhalant Prevention Coalition	800-269-4237	www.inhalants.com
National PTA Drug and Alcohol Abuse Prevention Project	312-670-6782	www.pta.org
National School Boards Association	800-950-6722	www.nsba.org
Partnership for a Drug-Free America	212-922-1560	www.drugfreeamerica.gov
Parents Resource Institute for Drug Education (PRIDE)	770-458-9900	www.prideusa.org
Stop Teenage Addiction to Tobacco	413-732-STAT	www.stat.org

STUDENT SURVEYS ON ALCOHOL, TOBACCO AND OTHER DRUGS

PRIDE Surveys PRIDE 166 St. Charles Street Bowling Green, KY 42101 270-746-9596 Fax: 270-746-9598	Student View Survey Johnson Institute 7205 Ohms Lane Minneapolis, MN 55439-2159 800-231-5165 info@johnsoninstitute.com
The American Drug and Alcohol Survey Rocky Mountain Behavior Science Institute 419 Canyon Ave. Suite 316 Fort Collins, CO 80521 800-447-6354	National Household Survey on Drug Abuse SAMHSA, Office of Applied Studies 5600 Fishers Lane, Room 16-105 Rockville, MD 20857 www.samhsa.gov
Monitoring the Future University of Michigan Survey Research Center 1355 Institute for Social Research P.O. Box 1248 Ann Arbor, MI 48106 734-764-8365 www.monitoringthefuture.org	Indiana Prevention Resource Center Indiana University-Bloomington Creative Arts Building Room 110 2735 East 10th Street Bloomington, IN 47408 812-855-1237 E-mail: drugprc@indiana.edu
Youth Risk Behavior Survey Att: Dr. Laura Kann Division of Adolescent & School Health Centers for Disease Control and Prevention 4770 Buford Highway, NE (Mailstop K33) Atlanta, GA 30341-3724 (770) 488-3202	Search Institute 700 South Third Street, Suite 210 Minneapolis, Minnesota 55415-1138 800-888-7828 www.search-institute.org

OTHER SOURCES OF INFORMATION

State departments of education

State/county law enforcement agencies

Office of district attorney

Youth advocacy organizations

School administrators' organizations

State school boards associations

State/local drug prevention agencies